DVD:
The Novelization

HERR DOKTOR MUSIKSPIELER

ROBOROTIQ

R.P.
PUBLISHING
V.10.1

Lafayette, CA

DVD: THE NOVELIZATION

Copyright © 2007 by Roborotiq Publishing

Cover Art Copyright © 2007 by Roborotiq Publishing

Library of Congress Control Number: 2007907866

ISBN: 978-0-6151-7135-7

Printed in the United States of America
(Exact location unknown)

From cover to cover, this is a work of fiction.
Any resemblance to actual persons, places, or coherent thoughts is strictly coincidence. Unless it isn't, in which case it still was (and don't let the abrupt change in tense fool you).

WARNING:
Reading this book may cause seizures
And it is not a viable form of birth control. It's effectiveness in preventing STDs, however, has yet to be tested. An unpleasant aftertaste is to be expected.

None of this material has ever seen publication outside of DVD: The Novelization.
Okay that's a three-quarters truth. But you'd have to ask Debi, to whom this copyright page is dedicated (due to her intellectual property fetish), about that and . . . well you can't, as she is not to be mentioned. To speak her name is to invoke the combined agonies of the seven circles of hell in liquid form and inject it into your veins via syringe while concurrently snorting methamphetamines and singing the Footloose soundtrack. It's an acquired taste. Also (and this is important), all of the stories contained herewith are about aliens.

To Milla Jovovich and Coca-Cola

DVD: THE NOVELIZATION MENU

<u>Feature Presentation</u>:

<u>The Last Words She Ever Heard Beneath the Cherry Blossom Sky</u>

<u>Chapter selection</u>

Chapter One	9
Chapter II	18
Interlusions: Oh Brother!	25
Chapter Tricycle	27
Chapter 14	32
Chapter %	36
Chapter 666	44
Interlusions: What Would Jimmy Do?	49
Chapter Ampersand	57
Interlusions: Give Me Some Skin!	68
Chapter ****	69
Interlusions: The Pain of Rejection	76
Chapter Nein!	77
The Chapter Who Loved Me	78
Out of Mind, Out of Chapter	79
Interlusions: Satisfied Minds Make Sleepy Time	82
Chapter December	83
Came a Pale Chapter	85
Think Happy Chapter	94
Welcome to Chapter Club	109
My Sweet Chapter	116
Epilogue: A Bad Chapter	121

Special Features:

Deleted Scenes

      I.   129

      II.   129

      III.   131

      IV.   134

      V.   136

Alternate Endings

    Random Endings   139

    Romathamantic Ending   141

    Ending too Hot for Hardcover   145

Scripts & Dramatic Shorts

    The Glass   149

    For Getting Things of Love, I Can't Remember   169

    Cancer   179

Previews   189

Autobiography   207

FEATURE PRESENTATION

THE LAST WORDS SHE
EVER HEARD BENEATH THE
CHERRY BLOSSOM SKY

♥ SOUNDTRACK RECOMMENDATIONS

Chapter One

"I don't wanna die."

She's been saying that a lot. I actually don't think she's said anything else since I met her. But at least she stopped screaming it. My head was starting to hurt. I guess maybe I should try talking to her again. I ask her if she likes cookies because I don't know of anyone who doesn't, but her only response is about how she doesn't want to die and I say, "That's what I've heard". So then I ask her where she's from and she says a place called "I don't wanna die". I tell her "I've never been there" and I ask her "is it nice?" It's hard to tell from her response whether or not it is.

She's in the middle of informing me of her great desire to avoid death (or maybe it's something about her hometown) when I ask her about family. Does she have any brothers? Any sisters? I regret asking before I even finish, but it does cause her to choke on her words and look at me. I say "hi" and then she starts to cry. Quietly. Oddly I find this to be rather comforting. I'm not sure what kind of person that makes me, I guess it doesn't matter. I try to think of something else to say and all I can come up with is how I got here, but I don't really want to tell the story because I'm not very good at that sort of thing and it's not a very fun thing to talk about. So I just sit and listen to her little sobs. I'd put on the radio, but there'd just be static and I don't have any CD's. Driving is pretty dull without music. I decide that I hate the silence almost as much as I hate noise. I start to talk. ♥

"I was on my way back from another dull day at work. Nothing exciting had happened for the last four months. I could do this job from home, but presentation was everything and I always showed up at the office in a collar shirt and tie." My tensions begin to ease

---

♥ **Manic Monday – The Bangles**

talking to this stranger in a strange vehicle driving across a strange landscape recalling another humdrum day in a humdrum life.

"The highlights of my day are always when an attractive lady find her way into my office for business related tasks, but I always imagined she was there for other reasons. And, okay, I know it's a little juvenile, but at least it helps to put a smile on my face and feign optimism." A grin spread over my lips as I recalled this to her, but vanished just as soon when I looked at the rearview mirror and came back to the moment.

"I skipped out from work early today telling my boss that my throat was scratchy and it was becoming significantly close to being a full fledged cough or cold. It had been a beautiful day in the city...

"I wasn't quite home when it all went down, but at least I was away from the eye of the storm," and closer to my salvation, I think to myself. I decide not to tell her about the "salvation" that I have stashed under my seat. It will only make her think about the immediacy of our situation.

I notice then that her quiet sobs have alleviated. Her eyes are swollen from crying and dirt and ash smeared her cheek, but otherwise she's in a much better situation than the other 99% of the population. If you consider death a worse situation.

I was pretty sure of that fact thirty minutes ago, at least, but now I'm experiencing second thoughts. And to think, the sun was so bright, no portent of this cluster-fuck whatsoever.

So let's go back to this morning, I remember that there was nothing unusual about it until I got in my car for the morning commute. Usually the worst part of my day, especially on Mondays, and guess what? Today is Monday. "So, Mondays huh?"

My passenger remains mute, I suppose I understand, but if she would only talk to me, this whole misunderstanding would clear right up.

"Listen, I know you don't want to die, alright, and I get it. But sometimes you just gotta face up to these things. Think about it. You're not dead now, and I can guarantee at least a few more minutes, so think carefully and make the most of it." Crying again now, just what I need. I was never any good at making people feel better.

"So this morning," I continue as it seems to be calming her a bit, "I'm in my car and quite unusually, I breeze through my commute. I mean, I flew, almost alone on the freeway. Was today a holiday or something? Didn't think so, at the time I just chalked it up to luck. Turn on the radio. Awesome, songs on every station. *My lucky streak continues* I thought. In reflection, the combination of these two unusual events should have tipped me off that this would be no ordinary day, but once you settle into a routine, especially one as boring and lugubrious as mine, it is pretty hard to imagine that anything different well ever happening to you."

I sweep my fingers over my "salvation", that's what I named her. Everyone was saying how unnecessary it is to own a gun, but I always knew it would come in handy. Not only for protection, but also for that charge I get from holding it. The touch of the metal grips in my hand is a reassurance that I can't get anywhere else.

Christ! What the hell am I thinking? There's a girl in the backseat, hysterical, and I'm off on some tangent about my "salvation"? It's true enough that the gun saved my life, both our lives. But I'm starting to sound like a maniac. If only in my own head. How long would it be before something like that spread outside of me? As crazy as the world may currently be, I still should work on being presentable. The world needs more stability not more crazy and I'm already talking to myself.

"Um, I think I'm done crying for now."

Odd, that voice was incredibly feminine. Why am I thinking like a girl now? Balls! We are actively trying not to be crazy, remember brain?! If I can't even follow my own explicit demands I might as well pull this car over and be done with it.

"So you don't mind if I, like, move up to the front do you?"

Now that doesn't even make sense, brain! And . . . oh! It's her talking! I completely forgot about my passenger. How embarrassing (you suck brain!). "Sure, and there are some Cokes up here if you're, you know, thirsty."

"Thanks." She's saying while she climbs from the back to the front. She's stunningly attractive (shut up brain this is a serious situation). But really even with all the cuts and the blood she's looking pretty fly (enough brain and did you just think "fly"? Those cuts are pretty sexy though . . . aw fuck! All is lost!). She notices me looking at her as she pops open her Coke, "Uh, hi." She says before introducing her lips to an unappreciative can. "Ah," she sighs, her face goes flush, clearly I misjudged the Coca-Cola's ability to reciprocate. I've never seen a woman look like that. I just want to drink her like she's drinking that Coke. (what?)

"Do you . . . do you want some?" she offers me her Coke, but I sense apprehension. (well she has been talking to us and all you've done is stare and—) And I never even said hi back! Oh well, I'm pretty sure the moment's passed.

"Any idea what's going on out there?" she's all buckled in now and so very pretty. How did I miss that before and how did she get so cogent all of the sudden? Not important, as I do know what's going on out there and I tell her.

I tell her it's Nightmares.[♥]

She doesn't believe me so I tell her again with elaborations. I

---

tell her that people's nightmares have manifested in a very corporeal manner and are wreaking havoc like nightmares tend to do. It's true. There's a long pause before she says "um, no".

Flat out rejection. And after I saved her life even! I'm not sure I want to talk to this tattered divinity anymore. I have trouble tolerating ignorance.

"Listen lady, I dealt with my worst fears this afternoon! Only in my worst nightmares would I have been able to imagine coming home to find my house on fire, with all my extremely collectible golden age comics in it none-the-less, and my girlfriend of two years fucking some Mexican midget! The shit that I have seen out in the streets is so goddamn bizarre..."

I'm cut short as the hood of the car buckles inward. Something large and wet glances off the windshield and the safety glass shatters. Good thing both my passenger and I had been wearing our seatbelts. At least there is something still fighting to stay alive in each of us.

When I'm finally able to overcome my shock, we're off the side of the road in a ditch with no chance of getting the car free. It's probably not worth it anyway, judging from that thick plume of smoke issuing from underneath the hood. The car's dead.

I lean back in my seat and let out the stale air in my lungs. I'm sure I've been holding my breath through the entire ordeal. Suddenly, movement catches my eye in the rearview mirror. The creature is alive and coming towards us. I look over at my passenger who doesn't look any worse for wear, but remains unmoving even after I yell at her to wake the fuck up. It's all on me now and the thing is already to the trunk of the car. My .45 caliber salvation is in-hand and I'm out the door before it even starts towards the driver side. My movement must have caught its many eyes.

Someone out there must have had a very active imagination to dream up this thing. A great bulbous lump with hundreds of black glistening globes ponders my unmoving squat-stance with gun raised in front of me. It must have some idea that I'm prepared for the fight because its tendril enveloped mouth hisses a warning before it springs at me with muscle-bound hoofed legs. Its speed is tremendous, but the .45 is faster. The first shot rips through the center of its eye mass and the second and third pound the creature squarely in its chest, knocking it back a few feet where it slumps to the ground.

You have to understand that one round from a 45 would knock any ordinary human about 10 feet back at this range. The creatures mass is incredible!

Green ooze, which I can only assume to be blood, pools underneath the dying beast as it gasps for breath. I unload the clip into it. Its breathing ceases.

The car is obviously finished, unsalvageable and there's nothing but open road in all directions. "At least it's not raining" I say aloud. No response, no one's got a sense of humor. The girl is obviously shaken, her face looks like a mannequin that's crying if one like that exists. Even with all the tears, her face is a little puffy now, but still, striking. If I save one hot girl from a monster in my entire life, glad it was her at least. I digress; the situation is obviously fairly serious. I can't deal with this for much longer anyway. I can't protect her, not if all she is capable of is crying. She's just sitting there in the immobilized car, the one that's starting now to burn, sobbing quietly. She's becoming a liability, likely to get us both killed. I'll have to address her gently.

"This has been a tough day, huh? Really, I understand, but we need to help each other if we're going to get through this."

She repeats my last statement with an incredulous voice tone, like she doesn't even understand the message of my words.

14

"Help, you wanna help me?" She says while wiping tears away, "You've done a real good job so far. I don't even know you, but you crash through my office door, pull me out from under my desk, and throw me in your fucking car like you're doing me a favor. Add to that, you try to tell me that the reason shit started going crazy this morning was that our nightmares are somehow coming to life?" She gets out of the door, her face full of a fire that has been absent our whole relationship, this morning. The car is on full burn now, backlighting her, goddamn, her body is to die for. That seems pretty likely at least given the current situation.

I say to her, "What had you hiding under there anyway? What was it that scared you this morning", a shy "nothing" is all I get, back to meekness now. "Must have been quite a sight, to put a grown woman to cowering under a desk."

"Shut up, you don't understand" she says to me, so I stroll over to the monster corpse and stomp on his face, I think it's a pretty dramatic demonstration. "Trust me, I'd understand, I have a plan, alright, we can make it, but we need to trust each other. What did you see today?" Yeah, I had her attention for sure now. "It was my uncle, the one who molested me, the one who killed himself in jail"

Molested, huh? And by a perverted uncle no less! How utterly cliché. (that's very rude, brain!) Yeah and I'd actually feel bad for thinking it if I wasn't so currently stuck inside some seriously disturbed solipsist wet dream. On the other hand, if a crazy uncle returned from the dead is the worst of her then that's not so bad. I did just shoot some weird monster thing, after all.

She's looking at me all weird-like. What's her problem? (maybe it's because you're talking aloud, brain!) I think I'm quite capable of knowing how to control my vocal cords, thank you. But oh God does she have the most piercing eyes I've ever seen! (what's that really mean anyway, piercing eyes?) Not important! Time to find a car. Or something better perhaps!

"Yeah, so maybe I could use a gun too?" Alright! She's stopped crying again long enough to talk. Not a bad suggestion about the gun, but I'm not sure if I should entrust such an unstable person with a weapon capable of killing nightmares. Of course, if she were to flash me a smile I'd probably melt like a . . . like a . . . (a lit candle?) Now that's the laziest simile/analogy I've ever heard. (I didn't see you coming up with better, but enough of that, she's smiling!) WOW!

"Let's go get you a gun!" I say. "But I still think we need a car first"

Her smile fades, and just as I'm reconsidering the whole gun thing she speaks again with that Siren voice "Well, how hard can that be? I mean, we're on, like, a really long road."

"Yes, and cars do drive on roads. Conversely it's a *really long* road."

"At any rate, walking is, like, better than just standing here. Follow me if you want."

She's just walking away like she's in charge all of the sudden? But oh my, is she pretty. (you might want to start following her, you know, with more than just your eyes). True, also she's seems excited about something.

"Hey, a car!" She says, as if I don't have eyes of my own. (maybe if they weren't so busy staring at her—) Enough from you! (I'm just sayin'.) Back to the car that she has now apparently gotten to stop, amazingly. (what's so amazing about it?) I wouldn't have stopped. (for her you would have) Touché. (it'd be nice to know her name.) Trivialities! Plus we tried that, her response was nonsense and DEAR JESUS there is a clown driving that car!

"Excuse me," I say as I approach the car, "Mr. Clown, sir."

16

"Actually, my name is Joe."

"Sure it is, clown. Now if you could just step out of the car." I request politely

"Um, what? Why? I was just—"

"If you'll notice the gun in my hand," I calmly explain, "I call her Salvation. See I like to name inanimate objects in an attempt to anthropomorphize them. And right now I think she's about to solve the world's Coulrophobia problem."

"What?"

"Christ, you are one stupid clown! Just get the fuck out of the car!" As soon as he's clear from the car I shoot him once in the chest. Who's laughing now, clown! (wow, that was pretty bad.) That's why I didn't say it out loud. (unless you did.)

"What the hell! Why'd you do that?" That voice is sexy even when it's scolding. (you have issues, brain). "He was just a guy in a clown costume!"

"Really? Or was he a terrifying nightmare come to eat our souls?" She's speechless now! "Besides, no way a clown could afford a Lamborghini."

"He could have stolen it!"

"Either way, it's not like we would want to travel with a thief. Plus, he was clearly a clown monster."

"You're crazy!"

"Oh I'm crazy alright. Crazy awesome! Now let's go find you that gun." She shrugs, says "'Kay" and hops in the car. And then we're back to following the yellow-lined road. (gah! I hate the "Wizard of Oz" . . . I hope we don't run into any flying monkeys.)

Chapter II

Over 100 miles down the road the N'sync CD begins again and I pull the lambo off onto the gravel shoulder of the freeway.

"GOD DAMN MOTHERFU**ING CLOWNS!! Typical!! To leave you stranded with only one CD and no working radio stations?!!"

I'm out of the car kicking dirt, rocks and any other trash off into the ditch. The girl slowly exits the vehicle.

"It's just a CD." She said to me.

"JUST?!!... It's *just* my worst nightmare! Well, second worst nightmare."

I reach into the Lamborghini and tear out the shiny diskette from its tray and send it flying through the air about 50 feet away.

"Oh, great." She begins. "Now what do I get to listen to? You?!"

I whip my head around and shoot her a warning look. Our relationship has been on the way out since she first opened her mouth, but now it's really on the straws. "There's only one thing that I can't stand more than these corporeal nightmares, and that's having an ungrateful little bitch back-talking to the man she owes her life to!" I pull out the gun and point it at her. "Maybe you're just another one of my nightmares! You know how I deal with nightmares?"

She staggers a few steps backward with a betrayed look on her face. I lower the gun and storm off the shoulder of the freeway and down the side of the ditch toward the vast nothing which stretches for miles in all directions. I don't stop there.

"Fucking bitch. Whore. Goddamn piece of shit!" I mutter to myself as I walk to nowhere in particular. "Of all of the end-of-the-world situations . . . I get stuck with the one girl that can't hold it together in the head!" (Maybe it's not her, jerkass! Maybe you're the one with issues, god damn brain.)

I kick at the tumble-weeds and rocks which litter my path, and then I kick the CD. I stop walking. Well, maybe it wasn't so bad listening to this crap. It sure beats trying to have a conversation with Ms. Shell-shock over there. I walk over to where the CD was resting and was leaning down to pick it up when the gleam of reflecting metal catches my eye.

It's a handle, like the ones you see on a gas station bathroom door, without any deadbolt or lock just sticking straight up out of the sand and rock. I pull on it to reveal a chain, long buried, which holds the door handle closed. I plug an ear and aim my pistol at the chain. It pops with the one shot and I reach down and swing open the hidden door.

Creaking and squealing the door drops backwards and stale air rushes from the chasm. Light from the afternoon sun penetrated the dark space to reveal shelves with many small boxes on them. I start down the stairs into the enclave and let my eyes adjust to the low light. Racks of rifles and other assault weapons stand dusty and unused. I pull one of the small boxes from the shelf. It's .45 ammo.

"Fate has delivered us to this ammo stash." This discovery fills me with optimism that had been absent throughout this whole ordeal. My plan is dependant on having plenty of ammunition. The other critical component is alcohol, which is of course much more plentiful and easier to find than ammo. You see, I've been thinking a lot about this curse.

"I was starting to have my doubts about escaping safely, sorry that I just blew up on you, it's been a pretty shitty day for us all. I have a plan and I think it'll work... you see, if people's nightmares are coming to life, then we just need to get to a place where there aren't any other people. That way, we're out of range of the bad dreams!

What's your name anyway?"

Standing uneasily, she just stares at me from the top of the stairs, not sure if I am going to fly off the handle again. "I'm really sorry for pointing the gun at you," I say in an effort to ease the tension. She's looking at me with those piercing eyes, angry.

"If I take one more step with you, I get a gun right? I am not interested in being your bitch, OK. If we are going to stick together, I get a gun and a say in what we do." I think for a split second about all the different possible (and impossible) ways that this could go all depending on what my answer is. I mean, we've already dealt with the conflagration of chaos that is the city, and we barley got out alive. But then again, even out here in the valley, there are less people, so not as much craziness, but craziness all the same. Well, who wants to go through the apocalypse alone anyway?

"Sure, why not?"

"Good, 'cause now that we're in this together... there is one giant problem with your genius plan."

Sarcasm is my least favorite intonation, especially when I'm not the one using it.

"What if either of us starts dreaming? We have to sleep sometime, you jerk."

So right she is. It's just that I haven't told her the second part of my plan yet, the part that will make it feasible. Casually I reach my hand into my coat pocket and pull out the flask that was a gift back in college. I always keep it filled with some sweet 100 proof bourbon; just a few sips will do you. She takes the flask from my hand and looks at me, clueless, like she needs it spelled out.

"You see, we just need to take a few shots before we turn in, and then there are no more dreams!" I can tell from her face that she thinks very little of my plan. Then I see her go for her purse and extract a tiny silver box.

"I see what you're getting at, and it may work, but valium will do for me, thanks. I guess we'll find out tonight anyway." We both crack a smile at this, the futility of our continued lives yet our desire to keep living all the same.

"So, I'm Victor anyway. I'd really like to know your name"

"My name is Gisela, and I swear my mom could not have given me a dorkier name"

"Mind if I call you Jiz?"

"You aren't serious, right?" Oh yeah! There's that fire I like to see on your face, you sexy minx! (oh, here we go again, at least answer the question.) Fine! Buzz kill.

"Then what should I call you?"

"Maybe Gisela?"

"No, no that won't do."

"It won't?" (it's kind of her name, dude.) Wasn't talking to you. (you're always talking to me) Either way, shut it!

"How about I give you a name?" (you can't just give someone a name!) Oh really, my parents named me! (that's different.) No it's not. And keep quiet!

"Um I guess that would be okay." HA! IN YOUR FACE! "But only if I can name you too."

"That's fine by me." Oh damn! Did I just agree to let her name me? Well! Did I?! (I thought I was supposed be quiet.) Quiet? This is no time for that! What if she picks a horrible and stupid name that doesn't at all reflect my crazy awesome nature? (I don't know, but you can't back out on a deal.) I know that! Don't you think I know that? You never shut up! (it's not that big a deal) Not a big deal? It's my name! How would she feel if I just changed her name (um?) Wait! Maybe I can get her to—(no way, don't even try) Silence! "Hey,

Emma." (oh balls) That's a funny sounding silence. "Yo! Emma!" Why isn't she responding? (gee, I don't know.) I'm so glaring at you right now.

"Wait, um, am *I* Emma?"

"Who else would I be talking to?" She's very confusing. (someone certainly is.) "Anyway, when you name me I just thought you should know that I've always thought of myself as a Doom or maybe Pylon."

"Um, okay but I think I'll just call you Victor."

"That's not going to work for me. Try again."

"Uh . . . can I—can I think about it?"

"Whatever. Just remember Doom or Pylon. Now let's get some of this stuff into the car."

As we pack the new found weaponry into our car like some sort of efficient packing plant workers (??? we really need to work on that) she turns around to face me. The day recessing behind her, she transforms into a silhouette and speaks. "Do you think this'll work out?"

"As long as you aren't going to start rejecting the obvious fact of nightmares needing to die by way of extreme violence. But now that I think of it, if you were all cowering from your zombie uncle, why did you scoff at me when I told you what was going on?"

"Oh right, about that. The thing is I'm kind of a compulsive liar."

"Really?"

"No."

"Oh . . . but wait! What?"

"Sorry, compulsive." Have I mentioned how perfect she is? (bulbous eye monsters, clown killing, general mayhem, and still you only have one thing on your mind.) It's because I'm an optimist! (the word is opportunist.) Uh-huh, and I think I'm falling in love. (I hope you don't kill her.) Totally.[♥]

We settle back into our plush leather seats and arrange our new-found weaponry in easy-to-access locations before looking to the road ahead of us.

"Next rest-stop is 50 miles down the road" I explain to her as I turn the ignition and this lambo beast roars to life. I buckle my seat belt and look over at Emma to see she is doing the same. Last thing we need is for that foxy dame to perish so early in the prime of her life by a stupid car accident. (Quit dwelling on getting into her pants you asshole brain!) I'm not! Just looking out for the safety of my new-found, uh, friend. YEAH! Friend!

I step on the gas and practically burn the tires off the car.

"You know, maybe I should drive. After all, I had just recorded the fastest preliminary entry times for this years NASCAR race," straight-faced she tells me.

"NASCAR?" I ask, believing her.

"No." She pauses, "I just told you... 'compulsive liar'."

"Right." I'd have to work on that. (Just like you need to work on getting in bed with...) SHUT UP brain!!

"But seriously, let me drive."

I don't argue. She drives stick much better than I. (that's just . . . I hate you brain)

After an hour of uneventful driving (uneventful if you don't consider peeking over at the drivers half uncovered thighs as she pumps the clutch when shifting between gears) Emma looks concerned and leans forward to look more closely at the instrument indicators, AKA dashboard.

"We need gas" she states flatly.

[♥] **Little Lies – Fleetwood Mac**

I dwell on this for a moment and dismiss it for the untruth that it is.

"Victor! We need gas!"

I lean over at look at the fuel gauge. She's not lying, we *do* need gas.

"Well, there was a sign back there that said 'gas' within the next three exits. But I didn't see anything at the first exit at all. It looked like a fire trail which had only been used by the local wildlife."

As I say this, we are passing the next exit which, thankfully, is paved. Doing 100+ miles an hour, I have little time to observe a defunct farmhouse which appears to be folding under its own weight, and movement between the pockets of moonlight piercing the broken rafters into the void inside.

"Did you see that?!" I yell. "There was something out there!"

Emma's left hand withdraws from the wheel to the automatic 12 gauge combat shotgun which rests beside her seat on the floorboard's trim carpet. "At least we'll be ready."

The bullet riddled signs show pictures of a gas pump and fork and spoon, "Next Exit". The ramp is soon within view, and we both see the tiny lights of a gas station/trucker's cafe twinkle like candlelight instead of the usual constant electrics of a maintained store-front. Emma reduces speed to a near crawl, cuts the engine completely, and rolls just off the side of the ramp. Emma swings back the folding stock of the 12 gauge and pumps a shell into the main chamber as if she had years of experience with the weapon, then pushes up the driver's wing-door on the Lamborghini and exits the vehicle. I have to exit the car immediately as for her not to discover the growing tent of my pants (Just whip it out and have at it!) SHUT UP!

As we approach the station with arms in hand, we can easily tell that other people are here.

Interlusions:
Oh Brother!

My brother and I sit uneasily in the loft of the haunted house, although with all the shit that's been going down lately, I guess every house is haunted. Jim sits across from me staring, eyes frightened.

He's only 3 years younger than me. Old enough to take care of himself, but today I let it slide. Now it's starting to look like he'll have to grow up fast. I need him now, not just to watch my back, I need him for that of course, but after a lifetime of looking after the sorry punk, I don't know if I can go on without him. I mean, all my other friends are dead already. I think. We're hiding here because there are things outside. I don't think I've ever seen animals like these, in life at least, but I swear I saw a whole pack of them this morning. They look like people from the back, but their faces are like a wolf. But with bigger fangs. Something out of a horror movie. I saw them tear through my neighbors. Fast. And strong as hell. These things have the bodies of people and the faces of ravenous beasts, like I said, and they run stark naked, which somehow increases the impact of their presence.

The things have been quiet lately, but we dare not sleep. Simply the thought alone is too frightening; it keeps us awake and alive for now. My plan is to stay awake, yup that simple. I know that we can't do this forever, but maybe if we do it long enough we can be spared.

"Bro, we got company" Jim says. Just then, a black sports car pulls up by the pump outside and stops.

"If they think we're going to fill up the tank and wash their windows, they are sadly mistaken." I say to Jim with a grin on my face. This is the break we've been waiting for. A car. We can get the hell out of here. Maybe down south by the ocean or somewhere else nice. Anywhere but here is just fine by me though. Eager to rush out, I grab Jim's shoulder. Fucking monsters, I mean, I never even thought about it.

"Wait till he gets out and puts the pump in, he won't have time to get back in that way. We'll wait and see if he's packin'. If so, I'll come around the back and shoot him from the blind side. If he isn't, well too bad for him."

I have never shot anyone, but I've been handling guns since I was a kid, know how to use them and I'm damn good with them. Targets, at least, pose no threat to me. This poor bastard will be my first, but fuck it, someone's gotta survive this, and I'll be damned if its some rich faggot who thinks he can buy his way out with his fancy ass car. My bro and I aren't bad people, don't get me wrong. Yeah we live in the country, but this isn't like we're into some Texas Chainsaw Massacre bullshit. This is just a bad time for everyone. We need to resort to extreme measures.

Anyway, the car stands silent, no one getting out. Just then the tinted window cracks slightly. Someone was checking the place out to see if it was safe. Looks safe right, no one around. Idiot. Soon you're fancy car will be my fancy car.

Chapter Tricycle

Well that was uncomfortable. (huh?) It was like no one was paying attention to me for a second there. (so? no one should ever pay attention to you.) Why are you always so bitter? (I don't know might have something to do with the whole nightmare apocalypse . . . and there's you, of course.) I am making the world a whole lot brighter. (by shooting clowns?) There is no greater joy!

You know what else is great? Pumping gas. (that's strange, but refreshingly non-perverted.) It's very relaxing. I'm just going to stand here all relaxed waiting for—

"Don't move motherfucker or I'll blow you're fucking head off!" That wasn't you, right? (nope, I try not to use such lazy language.) Yeah, you are more civil, so it must be one of them.

"T-t-turn around or you're d-dead! . . . motherfucker!" And that's the other one. From the sound of his voice he must be pretty young. (and nervous, what should we do?) Hold on, I'll ask.

"Excuse me gentlemen, but which is it?" (see, why couldn't they have approached us with that kind of politeness?) Savages.

"What the fuck you mean motherfucker!?" That was the first voice, right? (yeah, he's much surer with his cursing.)

"Well, number 1 you told me to stay still or die whereas number 2 said to turn around or die. So what I'm asking is which will make me not die presently?"

"We want you to, um, hold on just a second . . . yo bro, we want him to turn around right?"

"Yeah, I-I think so?"

"Okay, turn around motherfucker!"

"Righty-o!" (righty-o?) There's never a good reason not to be personable and pleasant. (sometimes we get along so well, brain.) I

27

know it! Now let's get a good look at these two rapscallions.

Hmm? They are pretty young. I'm betting the bigger guy is number 1. Let me find out. "Hey."

"Yo! Shut the fuck up motherfucker!" Yeah, that's number 1 alright. (and hey! He's got a big old number one on his shirt.) How wonderfully serendipitous! "Listen motherfucker! Give us your motherfuckin' keys!"

"What keys?"

"Th-th-the keys to the car . . . motherfucker!" Oh number 2, you are so precious! (???) "So hand'em over br-I mean, um, mother-fucker!"

"I don't have any keys."

"Bullshit you lying motherfucker!"

"Actually, he's just crazy. I'm the liar." Look at Emma! So in charge and all decked with shotgun. "And I can't believe you two morons didn't notice that he got out of the passenger side of the car." She's an angel! (that actually sounded sincere, I mean no sexual innuendo at all.) She's not an object, she's a person. She's Emma T. Thundercat, professional angel. (Thundercat?) That's her last name. (and the T?) Stands for The. (extraordinarily, this means you are actually showing growth, brain.) "Now I want you two boys to drop your guns and kindly drop to the ground. Please." And she's so polite too! I think I'll just sit back and watch.

Weaponless and on the ground, Number 1 chooses to speak again "Look, we weren't gonna do nothin' but take the motherfucking car. We needed out of this town."

"And we never wanted to be in this town. By the way, you're a crap liar so don't even try. We saw you from about a mile away lounging in your house and we heard every word you said once we pulled up. I mean, if you are plotting to rob and kill someone you'd think you'd learn to whisper. Or at least not yell. Closing your window might help too."

Completely emasculated, Number 1 continues, "O-okay then, but can I at least turn on to my back?"

"Fine," she says. "But keep your hands behind your head," and he complies. "Now what are you trying to run from?

"These monster motherfuckers." Well that clears that up.

"Well that clears that up," OH MY GOD! She just said what I was thinking, did you hear that? (of course I heard that.) Well get excited man! It. Was. Awesome! (it wasn't that cool.) Oh yeah, *right*. "Maybe you could be more descriptive, perhaps."

"Fine, bit—I mean hon—um, fine. They're like naked men with wolf heads just l-l-l-like--"

"Like naked men with wolf heads?"

Sorry I have to interject here. "Actually what I think he's trying to say is that they look a lot like that thing behind you." And with that she spins around with immaculate grace and fires. Silent like a butterfly. Deadly like a killer butterfly. The monster's head is instantly vaporized just like a cartoon. (except for the blood and the brain and bone.) Yeah, but with the head gone we are only left with the naked man parts. My disappointment knows no bounds.

"Wow, nice shooting girl! But there are dozens of those around just like my dreams, so can we get out of here?"

"Wait these are your nightmares?"

"I guess, yeah, so let's go"

"Oh no! Here comes another one!"

"What? Where's the motherfucker?"

"No! My gun's jammed! NO!" Interesting, what's this about then. (should we get up and help?) I don't see anything, let's just keep watching. "Jesus! It's killing him! Come on you stupid gun! COME

29

ON!" BLAM! (why'd you do that?) I was illustrating the sound a gun makes. It's called onomatopoeia. (I know, but I could hear the shot.) BLAM!

"W-w-what's going on?!" Poor Number 2, I forgot about him.

"I'm sorry, but the monsters got your friend."

"What!" he screams as he jumps to his feet, "they got my brother?" Uh-oh! He's looking at the body now: "Wait, no they didn't! You shot him!"

"Yeah, no. It was the monsters." I believe her, she wouldn't lie. (never.)

"You killed him! You bitch!"

Time to interfere again: "Hey, Number 2."

"My name is Jim and she—"

"Yeah whatever Number 2, just relax," a nice pat on the back should suffice. "Let's face it little buddy, your brother was a motherfucker."

Okay this is an awkward silence, I have to break it. I have to! (just let the kid take his time. See he's about to say something.)

"Well yeah, I guess that's true. . . So the monsters got him, huh?"

"Absolutely. If it'll make you feel better you can be Number 1 now. So can we crash at your place tonight?"

"Uh? Sure! Who wants dinner?"

Surprisingly, the nudist werewolf tastes pretty good cooked over an open flame. And with a nice cold Coca-Cola to wash it down, good becomes great. Add to that the spices that Jim provides for us all and we feast like gods. Emma The Thundercat devours her cooked man thigh like she hasn't eaten in days. (I'd eat her like I hadn't eaten in... never mind).

She catches me staring at her from behind the humorous I'd been chewing on. "Uh, I'd been meaning to ask... (think of something quickly! Ask her if she'll go for a pizza and a fu-SHUT THE HELL UP BRAIN!) ...will you be sitting on my lap for the car ride tomorrow? After all, it's only a two-seater."

"No. I figured you'd get more, like, pleasure from sitting on Jimmy's lap and talking about whatever pops up?"[♥]

(I'm shocked! SHOCKED! That Thunderpussy made a sexual innuendo! And funny!)

"Um. OK. I think you two are really weird. Also, I can um . . . do stuff. My brother showed me how to use most of the tools in the shop."

"Are you saying that I won't have to sit on your lap Jimmy?"

"Pretty much!" With that Jim leaps to his feet and runs from the light of the campfire to the garage.

Now is my moment! Alone, sitting by the soft flickering light of the fire with this tigress! I pull out a flask of spiced rum and offer Emma a sip.

"Remember your plan? You get the booze and I get the chemicals. Or are you trying to get me drunk?"

Is she flirting with me? I take a swig from the flask and close my eyes as the rum burns down my throat. "OK. I'll admit, it was a weak attempt, but under the circumstances..." I can't hide the grin that's spreading over my face.

But she returns the smile! Oh what a smile! Like a playful kitten, she puts her hand to her face and lets her hair fall forward to hide her smile from me. "Maybe just a sip to help wash down this valium..."

[♥] I Wanna Sex You Up – Color Me Badd

CHAPTER 14

I awaken with a headache. The dull throb thumping to the sound of a generator. The room is not very big, but manages to fit a full queen sized mattress into the space. There is minimal decoration. A portrait of Jesus hangs on the wall closest to the foot of the bed. Yellowing curtains glow in the light of the morning sun. A few moth-eaten clothes hang in the door-less closet while my clothes are scattered all around.

Suddenly full consciousness comes back to me and, remembering last night, I run out the bedroom door. Emma is standing at the kitchen's counter top looking out the window toward the garage. She turns as she hears me take a seat at the rickety table in the center of the space. She leans back against the counter and faces me.

"No nightmares I hope?" She asks with a smile. "Jimmy's been out there all night," she explains, changing the topic, "he started the generator early this morning and I've heard nothing but power tools since. What do you think he's up to?"

"Adding a third seat, no doubt. But I don't think we'll need it anymore. You can sit on my lap!"

She walks over to the table and leans in close, "You'd like that wouldn't you, pervert. But no. I'm still driving."

"I think I was the one doing the driving last night." (OH! What a come-back!)

"I don't want to be the first to burst your bubble, but..." She doesn't finish, just smiles that gorgeous smile and I can't help but smile back.

We both turn our heads at the sound of a heavy piece of metal dropping on concrete from the direction of the garage. "I'm very curious to see what Jimmy has stayed awake all night working to accomplish."

"Well since he turned on the generator, we've had running water. And it's hot! Now may be the last time you see a hot shower for a while."

"I guess my curiosity will have to wait. Lead me to the hot-springs!"

She takes me out through the side door and down a little hallway and through the door on the left. I close the door behind us and enjoy possibly the last (and hottest) shower of my life.

After we're both dressed, we go out to the garage, anxious for the sight we're about to behold.

Jimmy has slaughtered the clean lines of the Lamborghini adding a cattle plow to the front, a turret up and behind the driver and passenger seats, a full roll cage, and aggressive looking tires all around. He has even created a mounting bar on the turret for the 50 caliber anti-aircraft gun which we tossed in the trunk earlier, just in case.

Now I have seen just about a lifetime's worth of craziness in the last 24 hours. This sight before me under any other circumstances of normality would have been a shock, a blasphemy. You see, I am somewhat of a car guy, or at least a car admirer, my broke ass could never afford one like the Lambo, but then again, this is not normal life. Normal life is over for good, and what's before me looks like Catherine Zeta Jones, naked and wanting it. Quite simply, it's the most beautiful sight ever.

"Jimmy, lookin' good man, you really know how to earn your keep." He looks up, obviously exhausted, but happy to receive praise all the same. I can tell by our brief meeting with number 1, Jimmy's used to eating a lot of shit. Thundercat is less enthusiastic.

"James, what did you do? We need a real car, not some road warrior stuff." I look her up and down, can't help but do that when she stands in her "I'm angry" pose. Jimmy is starting to fade; he doesn't take criticism too well. We're going to need friends like Jimmy; I sure as hell can't build anything.

"T.C., I think I'm going to have to interject on behalf of Jimbo here. You see, what we need now, exactly what we need, is some road warrior shit. The Lambo, being the sexual beast that it is, now has the fangs to match." The speech that was so stirring in my malnourished and hung-over brain begins to take hold on my companions. Jimmy perks right up, and I can tell that Jiz was starting to warm to it also.

"Do you have ammo for the .50?" She asks.

"Yup, two cases in this compartment I built here and a whole trunk full of the rest. I built this storage area behind the engine compartment so that we can actually carry stuff too."

There is nothing quite like the sight of self satisfaction. "Jimmy, I don't know how else to put this other than you, my friend, are a genius." We share a laugh at this; the boy who looked about two points above retarded is capable of such utility and creativity. I'm somewhat sad at the realization that I really did kill Jimmy's brother, and now he looks at me this way. Sooner or later, I'll probably have to kill him. He's not too sharp, but he's got skills, and I'm sure that he isn't so stupid that he can't realize how gorgeous Gisela is. I see smoke in the distance, and decide that the direction we need to be heading is away from it.

Driving south, I realize that the craziness has significantly diminished. I can't understand why, is it over? No, unlikely. I turn on the radio, still no news. How can something like this happen so rapidly and with no warning? Then it hits me like a cold wave. I know now why there is so much less destruction. The farther we go, the more sure

I am.

"What's your worst nightmare?" This question is posed matter-of-fact, with no other accompanying conversation. Gisela brushes it off like I'm joking. No joke babe, 'fraid it's down to this. "What is your worst nightmare?" I repeat, this time in my serious voice.

"Why are you asking me this now? We've been over this, when I was 11 my Uncle sodomized me, and throughout my whole life I have had nightmares about it. Funny thing is the only guys I fall for are the ones who treat me like dirt . . . Babe." Good she hasn't lost her sense of humor.

"Look, I'm not Dr. Phil, OK? I am just asking you plain and simple, what is your worst nightmare?" I can tell she doesn't get it. Jimmy chimes in.

"You mean like the naked wolf guys?"

"No Jim, not the naked guys, why do you think you dream of that anyway?" Jim stays quiet. "Look, haven't you guys noticed that we've been in the clear for the like the last 30 miles or so? Don't you think that's a little weird?"

"What do you mean Vic?" Gisela, with her perfect mouth.

"What is everyone afraid of the most?"

"Dyin'?"Said Jimmy.

"Jimmy, you are right again. People are scared of dying. Our nightmares are somehow coming true. Everyone, it looks like for this area at least, everyone who went to sleep last night, their nightmares came true. They died."

Chapter %

"Okay, let's go in, get what we need, and get back on the road." Our little Emma is so in control now. Do you ever miss the crying? (no, why? Don't tell me you do.) Um, no! I was totally going to say no too, but I was just checking that we're on the same page. (*right.*)

It's nice to be out of the car, at least. Everyone's so quiet and depressing lately. (I don't think they liked your <u>Nightmare on Elm Street</u> joke.) It wasn't a <u>Nightmare on Elm Street</u> joke! It was a cautionary campfire type story with overt anti-smoking and abstinence undertones! (well, I'd hardly call it a story.) I'd hardly call your face a story! HA! (let's just get to looting, alright.) Cool! What do we need? (food.) Overrated! Next. (I don't know, how about food?) Excellent idea! We shall start with cookies and Cokes!

"Um guys . . . guys I think you should get over here and see this!" Is that Number 1? (I thought he was Number 2?) He got promoted, keep up! (oh yeah, then that's him.) It sounds like he's in the produce section. (we've been here for two minutes; you can't possibly know where the produce section is.) To the produce section!♥

(there he is!) In the *produce* section. (I don't want to hear it.) Emma's already there, probably because she didn't have anyone questioning her cognitive abilities. (shut up, brain.)

What are they looking at? (I don't know.) Do you think it might be corn? (I think . . . I think it's a robot?) Robot corn? (don't talk to me anymore.) Fine, I'll talk to my friends!

"So what are we looking at?" I ask.

"A Robot," says Number 1, "and it's playing "Mr. Roboto" . . . I think?" I'm not sure I trust him.

"Emma?" I ask.

♥ **Mr. Roboto - Styx**

36

"I'm pretty sure he's right," she says.

"Pretty sure?" Well that's good enough for me. (or you could have just looked at it.) Still, maybe I should ask, "hey you, robotic looking thing. Are you a robot?" Ah-ha! The music seems to have stopped, at least

"GREETINGS TRAVELERS. I AM THE ROBORACLE," responds the Roboracle.

"Okay," I say, "but are you a robot or not?"

"I AM THE ROBORACLE AND YOU HAVE COME SEEKING KNOWLEDGE."

"Not really, I was just seeking cookies."

"YOU HAVE COME SEEKING KNOWLEDGE. KNOWLEDGE OF ANSWERS. ANSWERS FOR QUESTIONS. QUESTIONS THAT PLAGUE YOU."

"I've heard enough, Number 1 shoot this thing."

"I kind of think we might want to hear him out . . . maybe." Number one responds in a very non-shooting way.

"No Number 1, shoot it." That should settle things.

"Actually, we probably should hear what it has to say," Emma says.

"Well of course we should hear it out. Stop being so trigger-happy Number 1." Why is Number 1 so quick to shoot? (I have no idea.) I'm guessing he had a poor upbringing, I mean that brother of his was a total motherfucker. "Okay Roboracle tell us things."

"I AM THE ROBORACLE. YOU WILL FIND ANSWERS OUT EAST. IN A HOUSE."

"And?" I ask

"YOU WILL ENTER THAT HOUSE."

"That's it?"

"THIS IS WHAT HAS BEEN FORESEEN. THE ROBO-

37

RACLE SEES TIME AS IT UNRAVELS."

"Well, could you maybe come with us then," Emma asks, "so that you could tell us what's, um, unraveling?"

"ALAS, THE ROBORACLE HATES TO WALK."

"We have a car." She says

"DOES IT HAVE AIR-CONDITIONING?"

"What's a robot need with air-conditioning? I demand to know!" I demand to know! (I heard you the first time.)

"DOES IT HAVE AIR-CONDITIONING?" Gah! (now you know how I feel.) Yeah, I completely understand why everyone hates the Roboracle.

"Yes, the car does have air-conditioning," Emma says.

"THE FATES HAVE SPOKEN. THE ROBORACLE WILL ACCOMPANY YOU. WE WILL DRIVE IN YOUR CAR AND LISTEN TO STYX."

"No way are we listening to Styx." I say.

"THE FATES HAVE RECONVENED. THE ROBORACLE MUST STAY HERE AND LISTEN TO STYX."

"Fine!" I exclaim. (and with enthusiasm too.) "We'll listen to Styx."

"IT IS AS THE STARS HAVE SHOWN."

"Let's just get back to getting supplies." I say. Walking away I hear Number 1 and the Roboracle continuing the conversation.

"So what other songs can you play?"

"THE ROBORACLE CONTAINS THE COMPLETE MUSICAL LIBRARY OF STYX." I think the Roboracle might be my worst nightmare. (just like you're mine.) Maybe. (do you ever feel like things aren't right?) Nope. (really?) Well, I have been wondering why I've felt hung-over all day, but whatever. Back to shopping!

Maybe it's by habit that I find myself in the magazine isle or maybe just chance, but it's the disarrayed and flaming books that first caught my eye. The corridor is littered with comics, books, and magazines. Little flashes of color zip across the isle between the two rows of shelves. As I draw closer, a tiny voice shouts at me from behind a bag of chips.

"Careful! The Immoral Many have taken control of my universe and have somehow found a way to breach our time space continuum and made their way here to conquer your world of giants!" says a paper-doll cut-out figure clad in the tell-all spandex of superheroness.

The paper thin cut-out flies into the air before my nose and hangs there, bobbing like a kite on the wind. "I am the guardian of the planet Anexia and sole protector of its denizens! My allies call me Entheus!" With his titular exclamation, he punches out his chest and places his fisted hands to his hips.

"Please, kind giant, aid me in defeating the plague of the Immoral Many before they scorch the natural resources from your lands and lay waste to the maidenheads of your virgins!"

I take a few steps towards the mayhem and pull a comic book from the shelf. After flipping through the first half a pattern appeared to me . . . every figure drawn in the book has been removed, as if by scissors! I turn to the little paper hero floating closely behind me.

"Listen, Entheus, how in the hell are a group of living paper-dolls going to take over my world, and where are these virgins you speak of? (Once we have the location of the virgins, torch these paper people!)"

My question lingers as I'm struck by an intense pin-prick of heat on the back of my neck.

"MY GOD!" cries Entheus. "You have just withstood one of the most powerful optic blasts in my known universe! What manner of creature are you?! Please, only you can help me to defeat the Immoral Many! With your amazing power combined with the might of Entheus, we shall vanquish these foes forever!"

"I'll agree to help you only if you will lead me to these 'virgins' that your fellow paper people are after. Otherwise, they can wreak havoc with only you to stand in their way!"

"What selflessness! In my travels through the 28 known galaxies, rarely have I come across such a powerful being who wishes only for the welfare of their world's virgin populace! You must be an inspiration to your planet and your name shouted from the highest peaks of all worlds in this quadrant!"

(I think the little paper man in tights may be mistaking my intentions, because I plan on 'inspiring' those virgins!) Whatever brain, just as long as we can get the hell out of here and back on the road!

"Okay. Entheus, I'll handle this debacle for you!"

I run to the hygiene isle and pick up some hairspray, and then I'm off to the front checkout area to grab a lighter. When I return to the magazine and book row, things have gotten much worse. Paper children lay ripped to pieces on the floor. Full comic books with hundreds of drawn homes, pets and people are burning on the shelf. Then I spot the first of the Immoral Many.

He is a large block of bristol quality paper-board with poor printing inks. And I never would have dreamed that paper could do the horrendous unspeakable things that it's doing to that other female paper person. I torch them immediately (although it might have been educational for when we get those virgins, right?).

I scream as a paper hand slices through my ear lobe. I whip around to find another hovering two-dimensional figure in front of me. This one wears black lace and leather like a dominatrix. I grab her out of the air, crinkle her into a ball, and toss her aside. How many

40

Immoral Many members are there?

Emma rounds the corner of the isle, looks down to where I stand, and skids to a halt.

"What are all those paper cut-outs flying around your head?"

I burn the Many with my make-shift flamethrower and respond to Emma while the ash falls around me. "Oh, nothing to worry about. You know... the usual crazy shit. First talking robots then an invasion from paper-man world. Nothing new." I return to my efforts of burning paper people.

"I heard you scream."

"It's nothing, just a paper cut."

Emma pauses, picks a box of chocolate off the shelf, turns with a shrug and walks away. I continue burning.

Meanwhile, Entheus is knee deep in trouble. He's been surrounded by three of the Immoral Many, and is now faced with extermination, or worse. They pound his two-dimensional form into a two-dimensional form with bruises. Then they pound him more. Holding him by both arms they pull in opposite directions. His shrieks are unbearable, but the ripping off of his left arm just sounds like paper tearing. Now is my chance. I snatch (heh heh, snatch . . .) the last three, crumple them up, and use my remaining hairspray to roast them beyond restoration.

I delicately lift Entheus, fold the stub of his torn arm, and set him on my shoulder. "Now you will point me toward the virgins."

Predictably, we take 2 steps down the aisle to the men's magazine section. A throng of tiny paper people rush out to give their gratitude; the Immoral Many has been vanquished at the hands of Entheus and his new friend the giant. Pouring off the pages of Maxim, a host of barley clothed female celebrities rush out to thank us. Of course, any other day this would have been a most welcome sight.

Today, it adds to my frustration. Someone had to dream this nonsense up, but couldn't they have just dreamt about having sex with the real women as opposed to pictures of their favorite celebrity hotties.

"Save your gratitude friends, as it was this mighty titan who made our victory possible." I hate how this Entheus guy always talks in epic. "Kind giant, I entreat you to rejoice with us, for you have set us free and saved our world." The look on these little faces was just to die for. I know now how Gulliver felt.

"You see Entheus; I have some bad news for you. Your world isn't real. You aren't real. You see someone had a dream about you, and now you are here, but you don't belong here, so really I have a responsibility to end your existence here." He obviously doesn't understand, because he just stares at me.

"You jest; surely I'm as real as you. How else do you explain that we are even having this discussion?"

"Well, let me just demonstrate this to you." I reach for a pen from the stationary section and scribble a crude monster. The sketch looks like what the Boogeyman would look like if he was drawn by Walt Disney. Immediately, the foolish beast springs to life and begins decimating the paper people population. The ferocity of the attack was amazing, like a starved and tortured bear set loose at an elementary school.

"You see little people, you are nothing. Your world may exist, as you are so sure it does, but by your rotten luck you are now in my world. And while there have been a few stunning changes lately, I simply cannot allow you and your people to survive here. You are nothing but pieces of paper, such an insignificant commodity that we actually wipe ourselves with it. So now you know why I'm going to kill you." With these words, the party is quickly over. I walk casually; my strides are about the distance, in scale, of a quarter mile to these paper dolls. None, not even the mighty Entheus, will be able to keep up. I walk past the outdoors section where I and grab a bottle of butane lighter fluid. The screams of despair sound like hopelessness as I'm dousing the whole section with fluid.

"Hey Vic, what are you doing?

It's Jimmy, concerned and curious.

"Nothing Jimmy, just killing the little people. Want to keep one as a pet maybe?"

"Nah, it'll be more fun to burn 'em"

"That is what I was hoping for buddy." With that, the match is struck and what would have been the most amazing thing ever to me at age 6 is now engulfed in flames.

"Hey, idiots! What's with the fire? You're going to burn this place down!" Gisela, so assertive sometimes, so hot always.

"Well, everyone in this town is dead, right?"

"Probably, but that doesn't mean you have to destroy things."

"Lighten up Jiz, when will we ever enjoy a freedom like this again? Probably never. You have never wanted to tear down a building for no good reason? Plus what are we going to do this afternoon, no TV so at least we can watch the building burn down."

"I guess, well, yeah you're right. Who cares anyway?"

With this, we walk out front to enjoy the spectacle of Arson.
"I HAVE FORESEEN THIS DESTRUCTION. YOUR IMPULSIVE-NESS WILL LEAD TO YOUR DOWNFALL. IN THE HOUSE IN THE EAST."

"Roboracle, your observation is post hoc, if you knew I was going to burn the place down, you never would have considered staying. Plus, can I plug my iPod into you? I have a lot more than STYX."

Chapter 666

(Wow, what's with the macabre fantasy?) I don't know, lately I inexplicably get sexy/destructive ideas in my head. It's called a coping mechanism and hey! What are you doing invading my fantasies?! (I don't have to explain the mechanics of our relationship, do I?) Of course not, just stay out of my head. (sure . . . what do you have to cope with anyway?) There were a lot of cookies in that store. A lot of cookies that didn't make it out. (so you imagined that you started the fire through a twisted slaughter of the paper people?) Weird, huh? (it's only weird because you actually did burn the place down fighting the Immoral Many, but for some odd reason you imagined going on a paper people massacre afterwards.) I guess I just really love cookies. And oh yeah! Cokes too! (I . . . I don't even—never mind.)

"Cool fire." Oh Emma, what would I do without you!

"That's an oxymoron, cool fire." (oxymoron?) Stupidstupidstupid STUPID! (who's the oxymoron now!?) SHUT UP!

"Yeah, I guess it is. Good call." Vindication! (I hate you brain.) "At least we managed to get a few bags of food out before it started."

"I saved some cookies!" I hope she likes cookies.

"I've never been all that into cookies."

"Oh." Oh my . . . I uh . . . what?!

"Sorry, that's a lie." Oh thank god! "I don't even know why I lie about small stuff like that."

"Could it be the compulsion?"

"That's . . . I guess I do know the reason then. Anyway, we got everything packed up and are planning to drive down to that shopping center back down the road in a few minutes. It's not as big, but it's also not on fire. At least I hope not." I want to pet her. (that's kind of sweet . . . or incredibly perverse.) She's just got really pretty hair. "There's sort of something I've been meaning to talk to you about for a while and now is as good a time as any so I was just wondering—"

"Excuse me!" What was that? (I think it's coming from our pocket.) Really? Okay let's see. Oh, it's Entheus. How did he not burn up? "Yes! It is I, Entheus of Anexia! The great holocaust nearly consumed me, but I managed to shelter myself in the hollow of your garments. I only regret that I could not save more of my people."

"And who might this be?" Emma asks now that Paper-Man is buzzing about our heads.

"Where are my manners? I am Entheus. Inspiration made flesh, champion of Anexia," he says. "And you, m'lady, even the Emerald Moon of Anexia is but a shadow to your splendor."

"Aww, you're adorable!" That bastard! "Come on over here by the car and we'll see if we can't find something to fix that little arm of yours."

"Truly you are people not only of giant stature, but of giant heart. Your kindness beams brighter than the Sapphire Moon of Anexia!" Would you listen to him! He can't even keep his story straight. (neither can you.) Stop defending him!

"I thought your moon was emerald?" Yeah, you tell him Emma!

"Oh, but there are seventeen moons of Anexia, and none do compare to your beauty." Where's my flamethrower? (let it go, he's just paper.) Fine . . . for now.

"Oh yes, the Immoral Many are a great threat indeed. But your champion, after withstanding the tri-optic blast from the sinister Triclops; and nearly being torn to ribbons by the dreaded Donnanatrix, vanquished them with but a wave of the hand." For a tiny paper man he sure has some big lungs, he never shuts up! (hey, he's singing your praises right now.) I should be singing my praises right now! (that's pretty self-centered.) Which is where everything should be centered! "Unfortunately those dastardly villains turned his heroics to their advantage, creating an inferno the likes I've never seen and truly hope to never see again."

"THE FATES HAVE DEMANDED THAT THE ROBO-RACLE DECLARE THIS STORY ENGAGING AND WONDER-FUL." Why couldn't the Roboracle have burned in the fire?

"I'm going to grab some cookies, anybody want some?" At least Emma knows what I like to hear.

"Hell-hello? HELLO!" And that's something I don't like to hear. (a new voice?) Coming from the bag of rescued cookies, I think it's another paper person. "I . . . I think I'm trapped in some sort of fleshy pit."

"Hey guys!" (Emma seems excited enough about it.) She makes me so happy. "It looks like another one survived."

"Astounding! And a woman too! Perhaps my people may yet live on!" Hey wait a minute. I recognize that paper girl.

"That's that little dominatrix that tried to cut my ear off!" yelling should terrify properly, "I'll have to crumple you up all over again."

"You are mistaken, friend," Entheus starts up. "The Donnanatrix is a feisty vixen always scantily clad in leather with her cascading hair and ample bosom on display in an attempt to entice immoral thoughts. This woman is fully clothed with pony tail and glasses. I should know as I've fought the Donnanatrix many a time."

"I'm sorry for the confusion," the new girl chimes in, "but my name's Donna. Donna Natrois."

"Yeah, you know what? Whatever. I don't care anymore." And

I don't. (who're you trying to convince.)

"Haha!" cackles Donna, "They have no idea that I'm really one of the Immoral Many sent to infiltrate and corrupt their group."

"Um, we can still hear you." What kind of freak thinks out loud? (I'm sure I don't know.)

"Hear what? I wasn't talking," she says.

"Okay." Why bother? She is kind of cute, I guess. Like the way she changes her voice when she thinks she can't be heard. (sure, if you like tiny crazy paper girls.) And I do. I bet they make great pets!

"The blind FOOLS! Mwhahahahaha!" Yeah, she's alright. (sometimes I just don't get you.) "And who is this giant metal man?"

"I AM THE ROBORACLE."

"You certainly are," she says. "I'm Donna."

"THE FATES HAVE SEEN YOU AND THEY DEEM YOU BEAUTIFUL." Wha-what's he doing? (I think he's flirting.)♥ Oh crap! He's playing "Lady"! This sucks! (were you going to ask him to play it for Emma?) Shut your mouth!

"You're not so bad yourself."

"THE ROBORACLE SEES PLEASURE IN YOUR NEAR FUTURE." I don't even know how to process that. I think I'm disgusted? "THAT NEAR FUTURE IS NOW. BEHOLD THE ACCURACY OF THE ROBORACLE'S PREDICTIONS."

A slot opens up on the front plate of the Roboracle's chest, not unlike a vending machines' dollar bill receptacle, and Donna the dominatrix inserts herself into it. Styx plays louder than ever.

"STYX, IN ACCORDANCE WITH THE FATES, DO DECREE THAT DONNA NATROIS IS THE ROBORACLE'S LADY."

The Roboracle's LED's begins flashing faster. His head spins

♥ Lady - Styx

around on its axis, and smoke begins to issue from his joints. Then it's over. The music ceases and Donna reemerges from the dollar slot whistling the Styx tune, but this time she appears in a black teddy and in mint condition without the folds incurred by the crumpling. She lights up a paper cigarette and little plumes of paper smoke disseminate into the air.

"Damn, Roboracle! What the hell did you do to her?!" (Stupid question. That's pretty obvious. I must ascertain the Roboracle's secret technique!)

I glance over at Jimmy who stands somewhat dumbfounded by this display, and then to my Thundercat who has that 'give-it-to-me-now' look in her eyes. (now is my moment.) I have to take control of the situation.

"So! We better split-up into teams to scour this town for any other useful remaining, uh, supplies. Yeah. Emma, you're with me. Donna, you'll be with us too. Everyone else, head that way. If you happen to hear yelling or screaming from our direction, just ignore it. We'll be doing it... I mean, doing it fine...I mean we'll be okay. Never mind, just go!" I grab Emma by the hand and lead her in the other direction towards a comfortable looking furniture store with Donna the dominatrix floating closely behind.

Interlusions:
What would Jimmy do?♥

"ALAS, IT IS AS I HAVE FORESEEN. SEPARATED FROM MY ONE TRUE LOVE AFTER OUR JOINING MOMENT OF TRUTH."

Jimmy tries to comfort the robot as the others run towards Soft Accessories Plus which neighbors a small post office. "They aren't going to leave us here. We'll all meet up soon, uh, later . . . I think."

"Noble Jimmy, there lies truth in your words. I vow to the Amber Moon, Sallo, as long as there be strength left behind mine eyes... I will not let our entourage fail!"

"MY SOURCES SAY WE SHALL ABANDON HOPE AND GO TO THE ELECTRONICS STORE ONE BLOCK SOUTH-EAST."

"Well, I suppose we could get some extra batteries for you."

"THE ROBORACLE RUNS NOT ON BATTERIES!! THE ROBORACLE IS POWERED BY THE WEAVING OF FATE ITSELF!"

"Calm thyself righteous mechanical ally. Our titan friend merely is proposing conveniences to our dire circumstance. He understands not the depths of your supreme intelligence. I shall lead the way."

The streets are empty except for the few tumble-weeds blown into town from a past wind. Entheus leads Jimmy and the Roboracle to the entrance of an electronic store, one block south-east of where they had begun. The chime of bells acknowledges their entry into the flat, fluorescent-lit space. Jimmy's eyes grow wide. He sets Roboracle down at the countertop, grabs a bag, and heads towards the back of the store throwing items into the bag as he goes. By the time he returns to the front counter, his bag is stuffed to the brim, and the Roboracle is

---

♥ **Karma Chameleon – The Culture Club**

gone. Franticly, Jimmy looks behind the counter. Then behind the racks of cell phones. Then behind the radio sets. Then he hears voices from outside.

"I shall vanquish thee as swiftly as thou hath appeared!"

"THE ROBORACLE SEES GREAT SUFFERING IN-DUCED TO YOUR CRANIUM'S FROM WEE-SIZED HERO'S THUNDER PUNCH!"

"A most sound judgment, my mechanical companion!"

KA-BOOM!

Jimmy dashes to the front door and peers through the glass. Twelve foot tall lamp-posts lumber away from the seven inch might of Entheus who floats above a street light imbedded halfway into the macadam. Entheus raises his right hand again, "And let this be a lesson to you all!" KA-BOOM!! His hand slams into the glass shade of the street lamp shattering its head and driving it another six feet underground. Distracted and panicked, Jimmy forgets about the overflowing satchel he carries. That is, until it starts to move. And as it tears open Jimmy can only think "oh sh—"

-Interlusions Interrupted!-

It really seems stupid for us to have split up; someone's bound to get hurt. Whose brilliant idea was that? (yours.) Right. Like I said, brilliant.

"It probably *was* a bad idea to split-up," do you ever get the feeling Emma's reading our mind. (that or maybe she's just not deaf.) What's that got to do with anything? "It's just that all we really need is food and water, everything else is just luxuries."

"I like luxury," I say.

"But we can just go live in any mansion we find at this point, right? Who would stop us? We certainly don't need to be looking for furniture. First we need to get this craziness sorted out, and we probably should have stayed together until then." She's always so right; maybe she should be in charge. I should tell her.

"Well then why didn't you say that in the first place!?" (smooth.)

"That's right, talk amongst one another," the Donnanatrix interrupts. (lucky for you.) "And all the while I'll be scheming my schemes with you none the wiser."

"Should we do something about her?" Emma asks. I think she's forgotten my little outburst. Victory! (whatever, just respond.)

"Meh. Why bother? She's just paper."

"Just paper they think," once again the Donnanatrix interrupts, "but little do they know the true source of the power of paper. Soon the Immoral Many will unleash depravity of apocalyptic proportions! Mwhahahahaha"

"Apocalyptic huh?" I say.

"What was that?" Ah, she's back in her innocent voice. "Sorry, I was just daydreaming about that sexy hunk of metal, the Roboracle."

"Uh-huh, let's just forget this furniture place and go find food," I say. "We didn't get nearly enough cookies last time."

"I was just about to say th—oh wow!" Huh? What's Emma . . . oh well, isn't that something. (what kind of flower do you suppose it is? It looks kind of like someone mixed their imagination with a carnation.) We could call it an Imagination then. (um?) "Look at how the colors pulse through its veins and . . . and I think it's humming, can you hear it? It's the most beautiful thing I've ever seen." (she's right about that.) She sure is.

The Imagination screams as I pluck it from the ground, and the colors freeze mid-flow.

"What did you do?!" She's screaming at me, she's never done that before. (I think you made her cry. Why did you do that?) I just didn't want there to be anything in the world more beautiful than Emma. Was I wrong?

"P-Probably," Emma says choking back sobs, "but it was also sort of sweet. Sorry I yelled at you, it just hurt."

"That's okay I just . . . wait are you reading my mind?"

"No," she says smiling, "but I can hear your thoughts." Whoa!

"I'm really sorry I just picked it like that I was only—"

"I know. Besides, something that beautiful is bound to turn out evil." And she takes my hand. Oh man, I can't think I can't think ohmanohman AWESOME! She's even laughing now and my chest hurts so wonderfully, this is the best moment eve—

KABOOM!

FUUUUUUCKKKKK!!!!!!!!

"I think that came from Jimmy's direction!" Emma says

"Maybe not," I say. I must salvage this situation! "Maybe everything is fine." KABOOM! "Never mind."

"YES!" the Donnanatrix exclaims/whispers. "The first plague has begun!"

"Like you had anything to do with this," Emma and I say simultaneous, and oh so awesome, -ly.

"What, of course not!" Donna cries back. "I'm just so terrified for my Roboracle. He's so dreamy." If I knew this would happen does that make me omniscient (oh god) well you don't have to call me that, but okay. By the way, who's Jimmy? (let's just go.)

"Soon we shall dine on divine sin! Mwhahahahaha!" Even so, I still kind of like her. (fantastic.)

Interruptions Interrupted! With Interlusions Continued: And then it gets confusing

Ever since Jimmy was a young child, he was fascinated by electronics. While lacking in overt intelligence, he is something of a master when it comes to technical matters. When his new friend the Roboracle joined their ragtag group, he was simply thrilled to have him. When the Roboracle suggested they loot the electronics store, he was even surer that things were looking up. No longer.

As he stands watching his new friends battle some imagined foe, it must be that streetlights resemble some villain of Entheus' world, he fails to notice his new Robosapien toy, is setting to work smashing his phone and laptop that were so recently liberated. And to think, Jimmy only picked up the Robosapien so that the Roboracle might have a friend. Jimmy isn't sure if this constitutes irony or not, but he really doesn't have time to dwell, lest the Robosapien's rampage will grow in scale.

"What the hell are you doing? Hey, Roboracle, Entheus, come look at this!" His companions arrive to witness this strange toy brought to life wreaking havoc on the store's merchandise. Nothing is safe from his wrath.

"THIS PRETENDER WILL PAY FOR HIS TRESPASS."

"Right you are my metal ally"

Roboracle and Entheus start towards the Robosapien, who ceases his destruction to momentarily scan his opponents. Suddenly, his chest opens to reveal four tiny plastic missiles. Jimmy has a silent laugh at this, until the missiles are fired. With all the intensity and decibels of the real thing, these tiny projectiles streak past the Roboracle and Entheus, flying straight into a truck parked across the street. The truck erupts in thunderous explosion.

"OH Shit! Run!"

The Robosapien draws his plastic light-saber and advances. "What do you want?" Jimmy asks desperately. The strides of the Robosapien are precise and measured. He advances at a steady pace and his light-saber hums.

"THE ROBORACLE HAS FORESEEN THIS ENCOUNT-ER. WE MUST BEST THE PRETENDER IN COMBAT. HE IS THE GATEKEEPER."

"Right then, we shall see how he fares against my mighty optic blast!" Entheus elevates as fire explodes from his tiny eyes. The Robosapien raises his light-saber and the mighty attack is deflected. Jimmy realizes that their robot foe is plentiful in weapons, but his size, about 12 inches tall, is his main weakness. As his friends continue to engage the robot in battle, Jimmy makes his way to the sporting goods store located across the street. The exploded truck had shattered the front window, where the golf clubs were on display.

Jimmy knows what he must do. He grabs the driver on display and takes a glance at the price tag. "I guess $3,000 is what it costs to knock a tiny robot's head off." Meanwhile, Entheus continues to circle the Robosapien firing his optic blasts while the Roboracle seems to be engaged in some sort of robotic martial arts. Now that the Robosapien is tied up, Jimmy strolls over and positions himself behind the little bastard, takes a nice golf stance and lets loose with a PGA worthy swing. With this, the tiny head of Robosapien flies off about a hundred yards down the road. The battle is over.

Entheus flies up to Jimmy, "You are mighty indeed Jimmy, noble of heart and brave in battle. Your story will be told for the ages. Never have I faced such a daunting foe. Yet you, with one mighty stroke, have eliminated him. Truly you are a great and formidable warrior."

"Thanks Entheus, it, uh, seemed like the right time."

"THE ROBORACLE WILL NOW INTERFACE WITH THIS PRETENDER AND UNLOCK THE SECRETS WITHIN." The Roboracle then connects to the empty neck socket of the broken toy and begins downloading, "SAVING TO MEMORY. 1% COM-

PLETE."

"Well I guess, uh, I better gather up my things so that we can be on our way when he finishes." Jimmy turns from the odd pair and begins collecting the devices and components which lay strewn around the shop.

"SAVING TO MEMORY. 1% COMPLETE..."

"Great seeing Roboracle, you must be attempting to infiltrate the most inaccessible of all secrets, hence I shall not continue to distract you with my very presence. Further, I must note that my speaking to you now does not add any ease to the difficult situation you now face. In fact, your auditory perceptions must now be greatly saturated by my astute findings and unable to process even the slightest external input!"

"SAVING TO MEMORY. 1% COMPLETE..."

"It is as I had imagined. Alas, I shall take my leave. God-speed, Roboracle. Godspeed." Entheus starts toward the door, but a faint glowing object catches his attention. Melting through a pile of debris left from the prior onslaught is the Robosapien's glowing sword. His small paper hand grasps the hilt and he stares fervently at the silverish glow that emanates from the blade. He stares intently, and perhaps would have continued to do so, if not for the figure bursting through the front entrance of the small electronics store.

"There better be some good goddamn reason why there's a lamp-post in the middle of the road half the height of all the others we've seen, and an exploded truck sending up a plume of smoke so black that it could give away our position miles away!! Have you no sense of secrecy and stealth?! We ran all this way to make sure you're okay and I find you here idly picking through a hobby shop, electronically cheating on your paper-doll fuck buddy with another robot," Donna flies speedily into the room at this, flabbergasted at seeing the Roboracle's inner workings plugged into another, "and

looking stupid and useless with your hands behind your back!!"
Entheus stands frozen, hiding the switched-off light-saber behind his
back. "I want some answers!"

"SAVING TO MEMORY. 2% COMPLETE."

"Victory! We have broken through their first line of defense!
The Roboracle has gleaned insights into the very heart of existence and
will soon unravel the very essence of creation! Thus he must remain
unfettered in this holy quest!"

Amazing. I try to spend ONE moment ALONE with my
beautiful Thundercat and what happens?? I've got to babysit the kids!!
I wanted some ACTION!! THIS IS THE LAST STRAW! (YEAH!
Now we're on the same page!! Go get some ass!).

"SAVING TO MEMORY. 2% COM—" A short buzzing
sound issued from the Roboracle as I unplugged his electronic sex
encounter with a strange robot. "DOWNLOAD CANCELLED! IN-
COMPLETE DATA TRANSFER! RECONNECT ROBORACLE'S
DATA KNOB INTO THE PRETENDER'S EXIT PORT FOR
ROBORACLE TO... tzzz... FINISH!"

"No more for you until you reveal these 'secrets' you've
discovered."

Chapter Ampersand

. . . . (um, you've certainly been quiet for awhile.) . . . . (we've been back on the road for almost an hour.) . . . (so, what's up?) Oh, now somebody wants to pay attention to me. (I always pay attention to you. I don't have a choice really.) Yeah, well everyone else is so caught up with this Jimmy character lately. (uh?) It's Jimmy this and Jimmy that. Well who the fuck is Jimmy?! (Number 1.) What about him? (Jimmy is Number 1.) That's nonsense!

"SAVING TO MEMORY. 98% COMPLETE."

All I'm saying is that there's me and there's Emma. Everyone else is just supposed to hang out on the periphery unless I deem them as worthy of my time. (you don't like Jimmy?) I don't even know him! (what about Number 1?) He's alright.

"SAVING TO MEMORY. 99% COMPLETE."

"Drat! The diabolically lovely Roboracle is only moments away from unlocking the secrets of the Immoral Many." Does the Donnanatrix have to do this every ten minutes? "I should destroy him but he's so beautiful. He's about to uncover our secrets. And by interfacing with another no less. Yes! I'll kill him. NO! I could never. Alas, I love him. Blast my heart!"

Maybe I should kill myself. (whoa! Hold on there, where is this coming from?) I'm just thinking it might be for the best. (I'm going to have to disagree.) It's not like we have any direction. (that's why we plugged the Roboracle back in to that thing.) We're just driving east, running from some crazy situation and just waiting for the next crazy thing to happen. (I'm not looking to die.) And what's that got to with me you selfish bastard?! Besides if I die at least this'll all be over. (or everyone will just pay attention to Jimmy again.) FUCK JIMMY! Everyone will pay attention to him over my dead body!

"Hey!" Emma! "Don't let all this Jimmy stuff get to you."

"Jimmy? Who's Jimmy?" I say. (I heard.)

"Okay, but we should give him his moment. He did make this car, well sort of, and we did kill his brother. Might as well keep an eye on him, make sure he doesn't build some super weapon and kill us all."

"It is what I'd do."

"Ha! Yeah I'm sure it is," she leans in close and whispers (must you narrate all this to me?), "that's why I keep an extra close eye on you."

"SAVING TO MEMORY. 100% COMPLETE. VERIFYING DOWNLOAD. PROCESSING . . . PROCESSING . . ."

"Well this could still be awhile." Emma says oh so adorably.

"Yep," I say oh so wittily. "So . . ."

"So . . ."

"What were you really doing under that desk when I met you?"

"Wow, sort of random, huh? Okay, the truth?" I better nod to let her know that's exactly what I want. And I do. "You know claustrophobia?" I nod again. "Well I have the opposite of that. Kind of. I get really turned on by enclosed spaces." No freakin' way! (dude, relax.) "Oh god! that look on your face is totally the reason I'm the way I am. Beautiful." Does she really need to laugh so hard? (probably.) "No, I just dropped my pen is all. And then you came barging in yelling obscenities and grabbed me and dragged me out of the building. I thought you were going to kill me."

"Oh yeah. That was awesome. I remember it like it was yesterday." (it was yesterday). Awesome. "You must be pretty crazy for sticking around."

"Yeah, but we did run into the gravel monster on the way to your car so I kind of understood something wasn't right with everything. Of course, then it hit me and cut me up pretty good and that freaked me out for awhile."

"I just hate gravel monsters. Thinking they're so much better than other monsters. But guess what gravel monsters? Bullets still kill you just as easily as they kill clowns!"

"VERIFICATION COMPLETE: HEAR NOW THE ROBORACLE."

"Ears open my companions!" Entheus is such a tool. "The mighty Roboracle is nigh ready to grace us with his everlasting wisdom!"

"THE FATES HAVE BESTOWED UPON THE ROBORACLE AN EPIC TALE OF PAIN AND SORROW. AN ODYSSEY OF TEARS. BORN OF WORLDS THRICE-WISE THE COMMON DENOMINATOR. ADORNED IN MADNESS. DECORATED IN PLAGUES.

"ELECTRIC.

"DECAY.

"DECADENCE.

"LOVE.

"THE FIFTH DAY WILL SEE THE ARRIVAL AT THE LAND OF CREATION. WITHIN AND BEYOND SHALL BE A CLEARING. WORLDS WILL BURN. INSANITY WILL PREVAIL. HOPE IS HOPELESS. IT WILL BE THE BEST OF TIMES. PLEASE TURN ON THE AIR-CONDITIONING."

"The Land of Creation! Then it is true! Mwhahahahaha!" I'm seriously considering teaming up with her.

"Me too," says Emma. It's like we're . . . (yeah?) I don't know, some sort of simile. Or maybe two awesome metaphors that go together really well. (so we're just giving up on trying to improve our wit.) Exactly, something eloquent, but not too flowery. I'm thirsty! Where are the Cokes?

I shift uneasily in my seat. It has been a hundred miles since I last relieved my bladder. Why did I have to drink so much?! The pressure continues to mount. Can I hold it longer? Maybe another 10 miles? No chance.

Turning to Emma, "You gotta pull this wagon over, now. REAL emergency!"

"THE ROBORACLE MUST WARN OF THE COMING ONSLAUGHT. THE PESTILENCE YOU VISIT ON OTHERS WILL BE TWO-FOLD UPON YOURSELF!"

I look over at the stocky little robot. "What the hell is that bullshit?! I should have kicked you to the curb the first time I saw you!"

Emma easily pulls the car over to the rough edge of the road and stops. I find a bush and begin to write my name in the dirt.

The ants pour from their hill as I blast it with my water hose. They carry their precious eggs along carefully plotted escape routes and I blast those too. Just as the queen finally begins her evacuation, a great wind rips a hole through clouds on the horizon and a beam of liquid yellow light pours onto the earth carving lines as deep as the Grand Canyon's. Other than seeing God pissing upon the Earth, what really catches my attention is that this torrential stream is heading straight for us.

I cut my respite short. Dashing back to the Lamborghini I have my Thundercat hurdle us down the freeway along our only escape route. It's hopeless.

The great stream burns closer, gaining on our position with increasing speed. Chunks of rock and mud spatter the exterior of the Lambo and the stale smell of urine infects its interior. The wave is

---

♥ Saturate Me – Mandy Moore

upon us before we can even brace for impact. The road in front of us disappears and we surf over the rolling hills at the forefront of destruction until the car loses its forward momentum and is pulled down by the undertow. The last thing I hear before we're sucked under is Jimmy screaming that he didn't know how to swim.

Starved of oxygen, I heave in a lungful to satiate my lack thereof. Emma's still strapped in beside me, vomiting yellowish liquid. Upward? A second passes before I realize our position. Upside down. I un-strap my belt and fall on my head. Mud clings to my wet forehead and clothes as I drag myself from the wreckage. I ponder briefly our unfortunate traveling circumstance before wholly focusing on Emma's rescue.

While I'm helping Emma disconnect her safety belt, Entheus and The Donnanatrix float through the passenger window to watch me work. Entheus is the first to break the silence. "Alas, I am hesitant to admit my one great weakness . . . I could not protect you, my noble comrades, against the treacherous yellow liquid! If only I could have flown our chariot to dry land. If only I wasn't so terrified of my ink running. If only I was printed on gloss-paper. If only . . ." Entheus bursts into uncontrollable fits of sobbing.

The Donnanatrix tries to hide the cruel smile on her lips, deceptively comforting the fallen Entheus whilst I pull Emma from the crumpled mass of the Lambo. Emma will be alright.

It suddenly dawns on me that the Roboracle and Jimmy are nowhere to be seen. Then, as if on cue, a scratchy voice erupts from behind a patch of old dead brush.

"THE ROBORACLE ___D GIVEN WARN___ __ THIS AVOIDABLE TRAG____." The Roboracle is half buried in the soaked earth with its decals peeling off from all of the moisture and speaking through shorted circuitry. The Roboracle lives, yet there remained no trace of Jimmy. The thought of Jimmy drowning in a biblical wave of God's annihilation causes me to choke a little from vomit in my throat. I can't hold it back. I vomit and follow that up with dry heaves for a few uncomfortable minutes.

After we salvage as much as we can from the tangled mass of metal which used to be our ride, I join Emma, who's wearing a make-shift backpack out of the Lamborghini's safety belts. She stuffs it with 12 gauge shells and canned food. I stare out at the newly formed valley dividing the once easy rolling hills, and try to make a bearing on which direction to head. "Which way," I wonder aloud.

"That way." Emma says pointing along the rocky scab into the earth. "We follow *God's* lead."

"It's strange," I ponder, "I almost feel drawn by some force to concur. I don't know . . ." I turn around and the sun is in full bloom setting fire to the horizon. Are we going to head East?

Again on cue, almost as if memorized from script, the Roboracle speaks, "I __VE FORESEEN THIS DESTR____ON. YOUR IMPU____NESS WILL LEAD __ YOUR DOWNF____. IN ___ HOUSE I _ _HE EAST."

"Yeah, yeah," I say. "Let's just get going."

"A__S! THE ROB___CLE HATE_ _O WALK."

"Don't worry," my Thundercat says whilst picking up the Roboracle. "I'll carry you." And with that we are off.

"THE ROBORACLE IS DRY. HEAR NOW THE ROBORACLE." Oh boy, here we go! (at least now that he's dry he's speaking clearly again.) And you think that's a good thing? (shut up and listen.) "IT RISES IN THE WEST WITH THE SETTING OF THE SUN. EMERGING AT THE END OF DAYS. FLESH GIVEN.

"BORROWED.

"WORN.

"FAMILIARITY BREEDS CONTEMPT. SALVATION AND DOOM ARE FOUND IN CREATION.

"DESTRUCTION."

"Well you're just a ray of sunshine aren't you," I say.

"ALAS, THE ROBORACLE HATES SUNSHINE. IT IS HOT AND NOT COMPATIBLE WITH FREON."

"You know, I think I'll just concentrate on walking," God I hate the Roboracle.

Walking sucks! (it's not so bad.) It's worse than driving. (I don't know, the car was getting crowded.) That's why we should have taken those dinosaurs. We could have been riding DINOSAURS! (that would have been cool.) Plus, we lost all our cookies again! (and Jimmy.) Who? (Number 1.) Oh, right. Emma's been pretty quiet since. (she also just tripped over that rock.) NOOOOO!

"Ow!" Emma yelps after tumbling to the dusty, but new, canyon floor. The Roboracle bouncing out of her pack, settles several feet away. "Goddamit!" she screams while clumsily kicking at that which made her fall. Tears stream down her cheeks as she says, "It's not fair. This shouldn't happen to people. No one should have to . . ." her tears drown her voice, keeping her from finishing.

What should we do? (just sit until she feels better, I guess.) Okay. (hmm.) What? (that rock she tripped on isn't a rock, it's a skull.)

"A skull?" Emma says, interrupting her own sadness.

"A skull indeed m'lady!" says Entheus with a graven face. "It looks much like the Opal Moon of Anexia."

Donna gasps, "You should never say such things!"

"I apologize, Ms. Natrios, but the resemblance is uncanny."

"Okay," Emma says, "what's the big deal about this opal

moon?"

"It's old Anexian lore," Entheus responds. "Nothing more."

"That's not true," The Donnanatrix scolds. "And you know it!"

"Either way," Emma interjects, "I'd like to hear the story."

"As you wish," begins Entheus. "It is said that, at Creation, there was the great Anexia, his mistress, Life, and the eighteen sibling moons (sixteen sisters and two brothers) that encircled them.

"Of these moons, the sixteen sisters were unique and beautiful. Lady Life rewarded them with equally unique and beautiful life forms. The other two moons, however, were more similar. From afar it is said they could have been twins, although one was larger.

"While both bleached of color, the larger of the two lacked the luster of his smaller brother, thus they were entitled the Ashen and Opal respectively. But still Lady Life was generous and willing to bestow upon the two the same gift she had given to their sisters.

"She came to the larger brother first and presented her endowment. He was tainted, however, and nothing but monstrosities did emerge, the only consolation being that they never lived long. Life was horrified and rejoined Anexia, momentarily neglecting the Opal. So too was the Ashen moon horrified. Disgusted with his station he conspired with the Opal Moon to overthrow the mighty Anexia and reap the bounty of his wondrous nature.

"When Anexia and Life discovered these plans they approached the Opal Moon, offering leniency in hope that he would discontinue his part in the scheming. Scared, the Opal Moon abandoned the plot. It was then that Anexia pulled the Ashen Moon to his surface and Lady Life buried him deep in the core of her beloved, but not before taking her gift away. Afterwards, Life revisited the Opal Moon, at last giving her final gift. Yet nothing would live on the Opal Moon."

"Since then the Opal Moon has shared the sky with his sisters.

But it is said that once in ten lifetimes the Opal Moon rises alone. Abandoned in the heavens he harvests his hatred.

"And a plague of death will rise from the core and walk the plains of Anexia. That's the tale of the Opal Moon of Anexia." How wonderfully allegorical that was! (um?)

"Would you be quiet!" Emma snaps at me with a whisper. Like I said anything? (well you did.) "Just shut up for a second, okay." And then to Entheus, "thank you for sharing. Let's get going. We've got a long road ahead of us." God I hate walking. (so does the Roboracle.) Well I hate him too.

♥

We've been walking for hours! When do we get to stop? (maybe never.) Horrible!

"It's starting to get dark," Emma says, right on cue, while taking her backpack off. "We should probably make camp here." I tell her that's a good idea and sit down. Emma seems pretty down lately. She must have hurt her leg pretty good. (or she's sad about Jim . . . er, um Number 1). You think? Hmm.

"Hey!" I yell and everyone stops what they are doing "Should we maybe say a few words about those we lost in the, um, flood?"

"That's a good idea," Emma responds with a little cheer. "Who wants to go first?"

"I will m'lady," starts Entheus. "Although we fought only a few battles together, I can say without hesitation that our fallen compatriot was but a mighty warrior. His heroism and valor do gleam more glorious than the Amethyst Moon of Anexia. I fear that it is for my foibles that he met his demise. I'm sorry, noble Jimmy. For the honor of your friendship, my gallantry shan't fail again." With that Entheus floats high above in an attempt to hide his very audible sobs.

♥ **Come Sail Away - Styx**

"Okay, um, Donna?" Emma asks. "Do you have anything you'd like to say?"

Donna starts in her cute librarian voice, "Well I . . . I didn't know him for very long. He was nice though. And that's why I'll miss him." At which point she rapidly changes to her maniacal voice and says: "Little do they know just how worrisome these events truly are to me and the future of the Immoral Many. The prophecy was clear, but with the ominous portent of the Opal Moon I may have to reveal myself to one of these giants."

"Thanks for all of that Donna," Emma say. And as and afterthought, "I guess?" After a moment of silence Emma continues, "I might as well go now. Jimmy was a good kid and well . . . he was a good kid and . . ." I should interrupt. Should I interrupt? (I don't know.) Yeah, I should.

"Okay! My turn! WHOOOO!" (subtle and eloquent.) "Now I don't know why everyone is so caught up with this Jimmy guy. It's too bad he had to die, but who I'll really miss is Number 1. He was a much better Number 1 than the first Number 1 who was pretty much a total motherfucker.

"He was a real pal, Number 1 was. A real pal. I'm going to miss the way he used to say stuff and how he modded out that car I stole from a clown, even though we never got to use that sweet turret on the back. And he was always willing to talk to the Roboracle so that I wouldn't have to and—"

"THE FATES HAVE ASKED THE ROBORACLE TO SPEAK NOW." This should be entertaining (dude, not cool.) Whatever, he interrupted me! "HE LOVED AIR-CONDITIONING. HIS KNOWLEDGE OF STYX WAS SURPASSED ONLY BY THE ROBORACLE. JIMMY WAS THE ROBORACLE'S BEST FRIEND. NOW LET US LISTEN TO HIS FAVORITE STYX SONG. THE

TRAGIC AND APTLY TITLED "COME SAIL AWAY"."

As the Roboracle's speakers begin to hum the melody he finishes: "ALTHOUGH YOU ARE DEAD. YOU ARE NOT GONE. WE SHALL MEET AGAIN JIMMY."

"That's really lovely Roboracle," Emma says as she scoots over to me. "Yours was nice too, Vic."

"No one's ever going to call me Pylon, are they?"

"Probably not, but . . . are you crying?"

"It's just, well, I really love this song." I say. And Emma hugs me and it's awesome.

Interlusions:
Give Me Some Skin!♥

The Giver stalks the valley searching for those in need.

There are many.

He awoke only a short time ago but already there are so many. He can hear another calling out.

Hungry.

Wanting to borrow.

It's dark, but the moon is full and the prayer strong. Finding the source, The Giver kneels down and picks up the caller. A skull. Beautiful and bleached. But in the pallid light of the moon he can see the remains of a dusty footprint.

How disrespectful, thinks The Giver as he reaches into his pocket retrieving a jagged stone. Already bloodied with his generosity, he stabs it into his left palm. Plunging deeper and deeper until the rock begins scraping bone.

He cuts upwards.

Sideways.

Down.

Tearing off his flesh, The Giver bestows his gift. The caller accepts greedily and begins to grow. The Giver waits. There is no hurry.

In a short while this Borrower will walk. Just like the others.

And he will follow.

Beneath the opal glow of night, The Giver smiles.

♥ **The Killing Moon – Echo and the Bunnymen**

Chapter ****

This ground is really uncomfortable. (you realize I'm trying to sleep?) And it smells bad. (word.)

"So you can't sleep either?" Emma asks.

"Not even a little." I say back.

"Can you tell me what I was even thinking when I suggested spending the night out here?" She inquires.

"Walking sucks?"

"Oh yeah, but I think it might be better than being out here, asleep."

You heard the lady, let's gather everyone up and get going. (good plan, I don't like it out here.) We've been in worse places, at least. (maybe, but don't you ever feel like we're being watched?) Never!

So here we are, hiking in the middle of the night. I suppose it'll be morning soon, so that's something. I'm starving, tired and still wearing the same clothes that were soaked earlier. The faces of my companions, even the ROBORACLE, reveal their relative displeasure at our current fortunes as well. Time for me to say something.

"OK, guys, I think we need a break. We've been on go mode forever it seems like. A lot of crazy shit has been happening, and I think that we need a serious meeting of the minds."

Emma chimes in, "Like Star Trek with that pointy eared guy?"

"No, that's a mind meld. What I'm talking about is the simple fact that we seem to know nothing about this plague. We don't know where we are going. We don't have food, water or any other supplies. And most importantly, we have nothing resembling a plan for when we arrive at this house in the east. We don't even know what will be waiting for us or why we need to go there. I think that its time we all sat down and contributed some ideas. Because this is serious."

"Aye, indeed we have no tactical plan of attack. We also are short one warrior. Our next battle will be won on the virtue of not strength alone."

"Thank you Entheus. Now first of all we must start with what is awaiting us at our destination. Roboracle, you interfaced with the gatekeeper. It's time for you to stop withholding information. We need to know about this house."

"THE HOUSE, IT IS IN THE EAST. IT IS WHERE YOUR JOURNEY ENDS." Roboracle stands staring up at me with his glowing eyes.

I look at Emma, my only remaining human companion, to jump in. She seems unsatisfied with Roboracle's bullshit too. She shoots me a quick "hey watch this" smile. Before I really register what is happening, she is holding the Roboracle upside down and shaking him.

"Listen up you little fucker. I have had it with you and your false truths, doublespeak future nonsense. Now come clean about what the house is all about and what is behind this mess!" Head spinning, the Roboracle speaks slowly.

"YOU CANNOT PERSUADE ME WITH THREATS. I HAVE NO SENSE OF PAIN. I HAVE NO SYMPATHY FOR YOU." With these words, Emma drops the Roboracle to the ground and stomps his arm. The arm snaps off with relative ease.

"NOOO!" The dominatrix lets out a scream that rattles my teeth; she strikes at Emma's face. A small paper cut opens on her left check.

"Ow bitch, don't you understand, you can't hurt us." She clasps her hands around dominatrix and holds her close to her face.

70

"Listen up, you are going to cooperate or I am going to use you as toilet paper. Now shut up while we finish interrogating your boyfriend."

I bend over the now one armed Roboracle and ask him again. "What is happening at the house? What is causing these nightmares to walk the earth?"

"The house is the key to unlocking your destiny. It is a gateway." The Roboracle is being uncharacteristically helpful. I am somewhat suspicious.

"What is beyond the gateway? Who is at this house?"

"The gateway is intangible; it is either a key to unlimited knowledge or a portal straight to your deaths. The outcome depends only on you VIKTOR. At the house you will meet someone you know well."

"Why do you now finally start talking straight to me? You could have been a lot more helpful earlier."

"You have already progressed exactly as I have predicted. My superior mathematics have predicted all outcomes down to the nearest 1 millionth of a percent. In nearly all possible futures, you fail. Your adversary's plan is fulfilled. And none of you live. I am restored as one who rightfully deserves respect and worship from those who seek my knowledge. I am Roboracle, and though I have taken the form of this machine, I have always been, and shall always be."

Emma asks uneasily "Why are you so talkative all of a sudden?"

"To keep you occupied while important pieces are coming together. You will find it harder to succeed. My lot is cast, you will lose." With that the light fades from the Roboracle's eyes. For the first time since we found him, the little bastard turned himself off.

"Why would he do that?" asks Emma. Just as she finishes her sentence, I know. I can see them. At least a dozen of them. Even in the moonlight, I can tell that they are not right. The group advances toward us, about 200 yards away. The wind shifts and I smell them. Like a freezer that's been left with the door wide open. Like garbage in the sunlight. I can smell them, putrid, disgusting and heading our way.

We don't move for a long time. Or what I assume must be a long time considering their speed. Fifty yards away and the paralysis finally breaks as Emma starts to shoot. My hands react unconsciously, responding to her actions. With Jimmy gone, the Roboracle offline, and the Donnanatrix attempting to turn him back on, it's only the two of us. Entheus stays back. He'd be torn to shreds by the gunfire. Whatever these creatures are they go down easy enough. That's nice, at least.

"Gross!" Gisela exclaims as we approach the fallen monsters. "They're just, like, mangled skin and bone."

"At least they're good and dead now," I reply and kick one of them in what I can only presume is their head. Just then they all let out terrible screams causing me to jump back and start shooting again. It doesn't help.

"They're singing," Entheus says, now buzzing about my head.

"Bullshit!" I yell back. "This just sounds awful."

"It's the music of decay," says Donna, who has found her way to my shoulder. "It's a victory song."

"Victory? Again I say bullshit! We just kicked their asses. With bullets!"

"They're singing . . ." Donna starts, "what they're singing is 'look towards the horizon'," and as we do there is no need for Donna to finish her translation but she does all the same. "We are not alone." There, on the edge of vision, stand dozens. And from that mass one emerges. It starts to wave. And although it's to far away to see, I know the figure is smiling. The screaming of the creatures amends slightly.

"Why is the noise different, Donna?" pleads Emma.

"The song changed. Now it's, uh, it's a love song. They're saying 'I miss you. Soon I'll make you mine . . . In the forest you'll be mine.'" With that the screaming halts and the waving thing steps back. It turns and walks away. With its departure, the remaining horde also turns and leaves. And I thought things couldn't get more serious.

"Well, I sure as shit don't know what the fuck is going on, but these nasty smelling snot sucking flesh craving meat-bags just gave us an opportunity to get the hell away from them, and I say we take it!" I tell my entourage.

We have walked for hours, yet the smell still lingers faintly behind us. It seems that even though we are not in direct sight of the zombie monsters, we are still being tracked and followed. We haven't lost them after all.

"Thou lookith exhausted." Entheus observes of me. "Perhaps it would be prudent to rest and restore our strength. We may yet have many more miles to journey before we find this much discussed *house in the east*."

"You have a good point there, my small paper friend." I raise my voice so that the others will hear. "We are going to make camp here until morning." I watch Emma as she finds herself a nice flat portion of dirt, unhampered by rocks, in which she spreads out her blanket for the evening to sleep on, and then I approach her, planning to make my own bed beside hers. "We've come a long way, haven't we?"♥

"Yeah. It's been quite a few hundred miles, or has it been thousands." Emma replies.

I pause a moment to reflect on the journey, but all that comes to mind is Emma. Emma kicking ass with a shotgun, Emma kicking ass driving that hot Lamborghini, and Emma just kicking ass all around. "Did you ever stop to think what might have been if this whole thing never happened? I mean, it would be better yeah?"

"I'm not sure I understand. It would have been better because all those innocent people never would have died... is that what you're asking?" She replies.

"Yes. But, I mean, have you ever considered that we never would have met?" I pause. "Sometimes I feel as if I've created this whole mess in my head, and the only *good* thing that my subconscious could come up with . . . was you. Or else I get so damned depressed because I'm happy that this twisted nightmare began. I'm happy! Happy because it caused our meeting. Happy because of my own selfish desire coming true. Happy because I found you." I turn to look out at the miles of earth that stretch out behind us. "I never would have made it without you." (yes, YES! Lure her in!) Shut up!

Emma gently reaches out and turns my head to face her. "Don't." She says simply. She leans in and kisses me, and I kiss back.

There isn't much around but we manage to gather enough wood to have a small fire for at least a few hours. The darkness of the night has finally set in and the two of us who need food to survive eat quietly beside the comforting warmth of the fire. Eating the small amount that we have rationed for ourselves really brings home the severity of our situation with this newer and more urgent problem. We will need to get some more food fast! I seriously doubt we will come across a grocery store, and hunting is out. We need the ammo to protect ourselves, not to mention the fact that we couldn't get close enough to anything in order to hit it. What we really need at this point is to have some more of those man-werewolves come after us so that Emma The Thundercat can shoot them down and we'd have some more food, or

74

maybe just find that damned supermarket.

Donnanatrix breaks the silence, "I think that's it . . . Got it!"

Everyone looks over in her direction to see the two orange eyes of the Roboracle light-up in the darkness.

"Oh, great." I mutter under my breath.

"THE ROBORACLE DID NOT WANT TO BE ACTI-VATED NOW." Says the Roboracle. And just as soon as he had been activated, he simply deactivates himself.

"WHY?! Why?" Donna asks the lifeless plastic toy. "We have destiny together!" And she leans over the toy and weeps paper tears silently.

Interlusions:
The Pain of Rejection

The Giver wanders his way east yet again, his Borrowers close behind. Approaching his Fallen, he lets himself frown momentarily.

A lost bequest is a brutal burden to bear.

But their sacrifice was not in vain. Any proper suitor must make his intentions known to his beloved.

Even if they are abhorrent.

Before continuing on his way something catches the Giver's eye. Although it does not call out to him he goes to it.

Takes it in his hand.

He retrieves his benevolent stone from out his pocket and, after cutting, offers his gift.

Nothing happens.

Hurtling the object to the filthy floor, The Giver fills with silent anger made vocal by his followers.

Minutes pass and calm returns.

The Giver once more picks up the item, placing the tiny toy arm in his pocket alongside his stone.

Looking toward the eastern horizon he can see a thin river of smoke, its current drifting towards the moon.

With a smile on his face and a new song in his heart, the Giver sits down and waits.

Chapter Nein!

♥

"You're falling asleep," says Emma.

"Probably," I reply.

"That's a bad idea," she says.

"Probably," I concur.

"You're going to do it anyway," she says.

"Probably," I echo and fall into darkness.

The Chapter Who Loved Me

It's too dark here. (you're telling me.) Is this all a metaphor for the darkness consuming my soul? (there's a darkness consuming our soul?) I'm just trying to be poetic. (but no one's listening now.) I'm sure we're not alone here. (it's just us.) I could have sworn I heard whispering. (it's just us.) Oh . . . this is a crappy dream. (I'm not sure it is one.) Either way, it sucks.

(do you hear that?) I'm not deaf. (just blind.) Apparently. I thought you said we were alone. (no, but this is new.) It's music. (I know.) It's incredible. Is it meant for us? (not this time.) That's good.

(you're killing her, you know.) What? (right now, as she sleeps. You'll kill them all.) I'm not. I won't. (not you, but you are. You will.) No. (in the woods she'll be hurt, can't you see it?) I won't let her. (oh God, the things you do to her.) I would never—(not you, but you will.) Don't tell—

I have to

Have to what? (that wasn't me.)

blood for life

Is this part of the music? (in part.) What?

promise me

I need to wake up. (no we don't.)

what you want

I need to wake up! (this has already happened.)

promise

I NEED TO WAKE UP!

"You are awake," explains the voice beside me. I turn expecting to see Emma, but instead I find Donna. "Morning," she says. It's still so dark. I can't find Emma anywhere.

Out of Mind,
Out of Chapter

"**W**here is she!!?" (if Donna didn't know the first ten times what makes you think she'll answer now?) Shut UP!

"It's like I said," she evenly interrupts (trying to calm you, no doubt.); "I was resting with my Roboracle when I heard you yelling about needing to wake up. That's all."

"Why were you resting? You're paper!"

"Paper gets tired too you know! Why were you resting?!"

"I was . . . well, um . . . Where's Entheus?!"

"You called, friend!" Entheus smugly exclaims while swooping down from the sky, holding some sort of package.

"And where were you?!" I yell.

"Why I was gathering food for my giant compatriots. I found one of those Soup-or-markets a few dozen miles off our path and picked up wondrous victuals along with the mighty Coca-Cola in which you giants garner strength," says Entheus. "Incidentally, where is the lovely Emma?"

"That's what I want to know! But you had to be off getting food!"

"I . . . I was only trying to help."

"I know! Now I can't even be mad at you!"

"THE ROBORACLE AWAKENS. REJOICE ONE AND ALL."

"Gaaaaaaaaaaah!!!!!" (whoa, relax.) You relax!!

"Friend, if I may," interjects Entheus, "I can cover far more ground than you. I will fly far and wide until I find young Emma. You must continue on towards your destiny." (he's right.) I know!

"Fine," I say, "but don't screw this up."

"I swear to you, not only upon my own life but upon the life of all of Anexia, that I shall return her safely." And with that he is off.

"THE ROBORACLE WILL SPEAK NOW."

"No," I say.

"YES."

"No! You went all crazy and shut down. It was one of the few pleasantries in the last several hours. I just want to know where Emma is, get to this house, and be done with all this crap. And why isn't it morning yet?"

"IT IS MORNING."

"See the moon and the stars and the dark way the sky is acting? It's not morning!"

"THE FATES SAY DAYTIME IS ON VACATION."

"Why should I listen to you after your whole you all die and I'm king speech?"

"THERE WAS AN OVERLAP OF SIGNALS. THAT WASN'T THE ROBORACLE. IT HAPPENS."

"Really?" I say, all with the sarcasm. "Because that's what he called himself."

"HE WAS ROBORACLE. I AM THE ROBORACLE. ALSO ROBORACLE IS A VERY COMMON NAME."

"Since when?!"

"SINCE TIME BEGAN."

"Whatever." I am so over this. (were you ever not?) "Look, why'd you wake up anyway?"

"THE FATES WISH FOR YOU TO KNOW THAT YOU WILL SEE HER AGAIN SOON. NO WORRIES. NOW THE ROBORACLE MUST REST. IN ORDER TO AVOID SIGNALS CROSSING. THE ROBORACLE WILL SLEEP AND LISTEN TO STYX. THUS PREPARING FOR THE IMPENDING BATTLE. IT

WILL BE WONDERFUL."

"Please don't go yet, my love!" cries Donna.

"THE ROBORACLE MUST LISTEN TO STYX."

"We can listen to them together!" she exclaims.

"OF COURSE. BUT LATER." Donna starts to weep her paper tears again. "YES. TEARS ARE STANDARD ISSUE WITH STYX WITHDRAWAL. IT IS AS IT MUST BE."

The Roboracle shuts off once again, leaving me and Donna the Donnanatrix alone. We begin our walk again. In silence.♥

♥ Ain't No Sunshine – Bill Withers

Interlusions:
Satisfied Minds Make Sleepy Time

The Giver stands amidst his many recipients. Two more have joined the mass. Although they have not borrowed and are unwilling guests they still must be treated with respect. It is a moment for celebration.

The woman, while defiant and stone-faced, put up little resistance.

She heard his song, after all.

The paper-man, however, destroyed several before finally subduing to the numbers.

Far too many gifts wasted.

The Giver expected such violence from the rest of the travelers, but not the paper-man. He was always so valiant. So kind. No matter, all is well again.

"Why are you doing this!?" begs the woman.

"M'lady," responds the paper-man, "I fear such inquires are useless. There is no reason within him. Not now. We can only remain ever vigilant in the hopes of delivering the secret to defeating this foe whence we meet our companions again!"

The Giver grows weary of the chatter. He begins his lullaby.

"No!" screams the paper-man "M'lady do not succumb to his enchantments." Nevertheless, the Giver can hear it in the paper-man's voice that with every word he's slipping further down. "Do . . . not . . . give . . . in," and finally, "Forgive . . . me . . . I . . . have . . . failed . . ."

The paper-man speaks no more. While all the woman can ask is "Why?"

They sleep and the Giver marches on.

Chapter December

"I can see something up ahead," Donna is holding a paper telescope that she pulled from God knows where. It's the first words either of us has spoken in far too long. (you don't know what you want, do you?)

"What is it?" I ask.

"I think it's a forest," she says before switching in to her immoral voice to declare, in an incredibly poor attempt at a whisper, "It's the Land of Creation! Mwhahahahaha!"

"How far away do you think it is?" I wonder.

"A day's walk," she replies. "Two at the most."

"That's fantastic," I say, without my usual charm and enthusiasm.

We walk quietly for a ways before Donna interrupts: "So, um . . . why do you talk to yourself all the time?"

I pause I need to give her a look. (what kind of look?) I don't know a weird one? "I have no idea what you're talking about," I say. (now give the look.) Already done! "But while we're on the subject, why do *you* talk to *yourself*?"

"I don't," she says simply.

"Well then."

"Indeed."

We thus continue our descent deeper into the east. (and deeper into boredom.) Nice! (thanks!)

"See!" Donna starts up, "you're doing it right now."

"Doing what?" Seriously what? (forget it man, it's Donna-natrix.)

"Yeah, never mind," she says before bringing back her evil voice, "Never mind these frivolities! The Land of Creation draws near. The Immoral Many shall regain our power! Mwhahahahaha!"

"And you don't talk to yourself?"

"I don't!"

"Okay!" She's fooling herself. (she's not alone.) What? (nothing.) Right then. Back to walking. (at least there's a nice wind at our back.) It's a bit moist though. (I think a storm is coming.) That's cool, I like the rain.

"Well, I don't!" exclaims Donna.

"You don't what?" I wonder.

"I don't . . ." she pauses, giving me a confused and, I think, aggravated look before finally finishing with "know?"

What's that supposed to mean? (I don't know.) Me neither! She's a very odd paper girl.

Came a Pale Chapter

Yes, indeed it is the beginning. Of the end, perhaps. Maybe this was all simply the end of the beginning. Oh, so different are these? No, but perception is everything. Perception, yes If only I can keep my mind together long enough. So tired. There may yet be time. For what exactly remains to be seen. This entire ordeal has unfolded to me in strange segments, broken chronology. And I'm so tired. I know up is not down, but how can I be so sure in a world where dreams come to life and nightmares walk the earth.

Hungry sounds emanate from my gut. I take the time to savor the gentle rumbling. Something about this feeling is always exhilarating to me. With my eyes closed I'm back home, my kitchen filled with the smell of frying bacon. Coffee, wheat toast and scrambled eggs. Of all the amazing things that I have experienced this past week, I would trade it all at this time for a hot breakfast.

My so called companions. Useless. An ambiguous future telling half truth double-speaker, coupled, of course, with a paper doll. One who thinks out loud. At least that robot has a sense of humor, or is programmed to, or something. I can hardly think. Are they even with me? They can't be, yet my mind . . . so tired. I can feel the grey creeping up on the corners of my vision. I . . . we have walked for miles through a jagged canyon, no food, little water and now, no human to talk to.

"Roboracle, awaken and enlighten us. Within you is the knowledge that is either our deliverance or our doom. I ask you now, what is awaiting us at this house? It isn't a house at all, really at least. I need to know why we have suffered. Can you help me? I implore you!"

His red eyes flash to life as he is reactivated, his head spins and he begins to speak.

"THE FATES HAVE DECREED YOU WORTHY VIKTOR. YOUR QUEST IS NEARLY COMPLETED. THOUGH MANY CHALLENGES YOU HAVE FACED, YOUR FINAL TEST IS YET TO COME. AT THE RIGHT TIME, YOU WILL KNOW YOUR PURPOSE. I CANNOT DISCLOSE TO YOU ANYMORE UNTIL THAT TIME IS UPON US. YOUR DESTINY LIES AHEAD. I LEAVE YOU TO IT." As usual, very dramatic and self important. And then he is quiet. His eyes once again dull. Can I trust him in this dire situation? Do I have a choice? I'm so tired.

"VIKTOR". I thought the little jerk had shut down, wait, that wasn't him at all.

"Donna, did you say something?"

"Why no Vik, and by the way, I wish you wouldn't treat my Roboyfriend so meanly either. Far better than you will receive. Mwha-hahahahaha!"

"What?"

"Oh, nothing. Excuse me" Quiet as a mouse. Bitch.

"VIKTOR", the wind licks my ear as she speaks my name again. It's her! Emma—I mean Gisela? She's not dead? I thought I—exhaustion and stress. Making it hard to think. If only I could reach her. I don't even know where she is. I though she was—where is that self righteous Entheus anyway? He can fly. He can find her. Can he?

"VIKTOR, he's gone for now, but he has plans for you. He has plans for us all. He can feel us, and now, I can feel him. You have to hurry, He's close by, and I won't get a chance to reach out again once he's back."

"Once who is back?" I yell at the starry sky. My companions, I suppose, have become used to this sort of behavior.

"You know him well, we all do. It's Jim, but he's not himself anymore. He's the one we saw last night. He's herding us now, for some reason. He could have killed me, but he didn't. He has plans, like I said."

"Vik, you're acting even stranger than normal, is everything all right?" little Donna asks in her librarian voice.

"Shut the hell up Donna, can't you see I'm in the middle of a conversation here?"

"Whatever, freak."

"VIKTOR SHUT UP AND LISTEN!" a much sweeter voice fills my ears. Is this my punishment? "You are the key to this all, why this all is happening, why this started in the first place. I don't know why, but he needs you. He just made me come to him to get to you. Don't give in."

"Well then what am I supposed to do?" Crickets chirping. You never really appreciate the darkness of night in the city.

"Where are you guys anyway?" Nothing.

"Hello?" Alone again. I wish I knew what to do, but I can't face Jimmy, not now. I think I know what he wants from me, and I am certainly not about to let that happen. All I can do is keep moving forward. All fear, all hesitation must be clear from my head if there is going to be any resolution that involves me surviving. I have come too far to die in this freakshow.

"Jim, I'm sorry, but I've no problem killing you again," I whisper into the air. Can he hear me? I'm tired. I can't make sense—I need to finish this.

♥

Without the conversation of either Donna or Roboracle I'm left to my own terrible thoughts. What the mind can create when you're

---

♥ Crazy – Patsy Cline

exhausted and almost at the point of a complete breakdown from heat stroke is really amazing. Dizzy images flood my mind of what that sick fuck who raises dead bodies is doing to my girlfriend. (Probably exactly what I want to do to her!) Entheus has failed in bringing her back to me and the only thing that keeps me going is some psychotic mental break which makes me believe I've heard her voice through a unique telepathic link. (Oh! So you think you can ignore me now?) I would have hoped that my mind would be able to conjure up something more . . . impressive. Why couldn't it have been a trans-dimensional portal to phase through the many planes of existence so that I could simply teleport to her? I don't want to hear her voice in my head. I want to make sure she's okay. (And then I can—) I can't bear the thought of all those rotting and festering hands holding her hostage . . . gripping her . . . touching her . . . (yeah, you're getting me all hot!) GODDAMN IT! I want this to end now! (Just give in.) But the only thing I can be sure of is that if I go to this magical hippy house in the woods, I will be reunited with my lost love. Oh Emma, why did you leave us in the first place? I need someone to talk to, someone who understands what I'm dealing with here. I don't think Donna will grant me a reprieve from the silence since last she spoke I chastised her for it. Maybe I'll just talk to a rock on the ground and let myself vent this frustration. (No need for that.) What? (I knew you couldn't ignore me for long, don't worry, she's enjoying it.) Who's enjoying what? (She's enjoying being taken so brutally at the mercy of hundreds!) Oh you sick fucking bastard! You say one more word about—(She's choking on their rotten meat, and when I say meat I mean . . .) I know what the bloody hell you mean! (Soon she'll be like a train station with all that traffic!) Where do you come up with this shit?! And who the hell are you? You've been bugging the shit out of me since this story began! (Just consider me your second head, you know, the lower one.) Fuck you! You've got some serious perverted issues going on there! (I have issues? You're the one who's talking with himself!) There's no way that you're a creation of my mind, and if you were I'd be able to simply think you out of existence! ...Vicktor? Hey you sick bastard.... VIKTORR!! Wow, maybe that was my mind? (Got you, you silly looking ass weasel festering in week old fecal matter! You should get that shiny coat of yours polished up by having some −) I don't even want to hear what you're planning on saying! Just shut the fuck up and leave me to my despair! (You don't know despair. Not yet at least, but you will when you go to the forest. Talk about an ass raping!) No one is getting raped you perverted shit! (I seem to remember otherwise! Do you remember that night you and Emma had together after first meeting Jimmy?) Yeah, we thought that nightmare's were causing all this craziness so we each took drugs of our choice to prevent our own dreaming and passed out shortly after. (Yeah, and pig's fly! I raped the hell out of her, and she loved it!) Stop it damn you! (Search your feelings; you know it to be true!) That's impossible . . . That's not true . . . NOOOOOOOOOOOOO! No. (We were meant to work together, to rule over Emma's taste for disgusting men TOGETHER!) I'll never join you! (Vikter, it's the only way—) No! There is another.

I pulled out my 'salvation', pulled the hammer back, put it to the side of my head and squeezed down on the trigger.

CLICK

(what was that?) Um. (WHY IS THERE A GUN POINTED AT OUR HEAD?!) Um.

"Hey!" shouts Donna as she smacks the gun out of my hand. (why was it there in the first place?) Um. "What the hell are you doing?!"

"Um."

"You almost made me break my promise!"

"And I almost blew my head off so were even. Wait, what promise?"

"Promise? Oh—well the thing is—you see I made this promise to, uh, never witness a suicide . . . yeah that's what I promised alright!"

"You're weird." Seriously, she's weird. (yet she still wasn't the one pointing a gun at our head after some weird Star Wars rant.) Empire Strikes Back, actually. (I'm well aware.) I just want to be clear. I mean at least our last words wouldn't have been about Ewoks. (I don't follow your logic. Ever.) Also, I'm pretty sure I had nothing to do with the gun thing or the Star Wars thing. That was you. (bullshit!)

"THE ROBORACLE LOVES EWOKS."

"Yeah, well the Roboracle can – arg! He's off again!" Stupid The Roboracle always getting the last word. He *would* love Ewoks. He's practically an Ewok himself. (uh huh.) No, seriously. He's more than a little convenient, really annoying, and clearly manufactured to entertain children. The Roboracle is totally my Ewok. (does that mean he's going to save us all?) It would be just like the little bastard to pull something like that. Just to spite me.

"Finally! The Land of Creation!! Mwhahahahaha!" cackles Donna.

Oh . . . I guess we're in the forest now. (maybe you should pay more attention.) Maybe you should mind your own business! So what now?

"We follow the path," says Donna without being prompted. (you really don't get this do you?)

"And how do you know that?" I ask.

"I don't know, maybe you could look around at all the signs that say 'follow the path: destination 5 miles'."

"Psh! Signs are for people who take the time to stop and read them—OW!—Why'd you throw an acorn at me?!"

90

"I didn't!"

"Well someone did and—OW!—there, you did it again!"

"What?! You were looking right at me, clearly I didn't do it!"

"Get out of our 'ome!" screams a voice from the woods as several winged figures swarm out of the forest to attack me.

"Oh crap! Talking bees! Get'em off me Donna! GET THEM OFF!"

"*Bees*?" asks a tiny voice as the bees stop punching me. (since when do bees punch?) "We aren't bees we aren't! Sayin' we're all like insects. The nerve!" says the tiny voice which I now realize is coming from one of the bees that aren't bees, but little ladies. Covered scantily in leaves. FAIRIES!!

"*Fairies*!" the voice screams as most of the other fairies flee back into the trees, "first bees and now fairies!" She's a spicy little number with cascading chestnut hair and an ample bosom. (proportionally speaking.) Yeah. "Hey! Are yeh touched in the 'ead or sometin'? I'm tryin' to talk to yeh."

"Then talk, fairy-girl," I say.

"There 'e goes again wit the name callin'," she says turning to one of her companions. A fiery red-head with sparkling blue wings, "talkin' to us like we're common gnomes."

"We ain't gnomes and we sure ain't fairies!" yells the red-head.

"Tinkin' were fairies," goes the chestnut one, "never in my 'ole life 'ave I been so insulted. Fairies are only the most notorious and disgustingly vain creatures—"

"—always spyin' their reflections in the rivers and flashin' the forest elves their goodies—"

"—and talkin' 'bout how bea'iful they look and enchantin' anyt'ing with 'alf a brain to come 'round and praise their breasts. Right sluts they are!"

"Oh," Donna finally speaks, "what exactly are you then? If you don't mind me asking that is."

"Wait," starts the chestnut one, "yeh aren't one of us." She takes a moment to examine Donna before continuing, "No, I guess not. Yer a bit flat and not a single wing. Well, never mind that. Can't yeh tell what we are by our accents? Wer sprites we are." Tell by their accents? (that's what she said.) But in that case they sound like a mix between French, Irish, and retarded.

"I'm gonna pretend I dinna 'ear that," says the chestnut sprite while giving me a wholly unsavory look. These sprites just aren't very friendly, I guess. "Anyway," she says to Donna, "if yeh aren't a sprite or pixie what are yeh?"

"I'm an Anexian librarian, among other things," says Donna.

"Wouldn't know 'bout that, I wouldn't. But I can tell yeh that yeh'd look fabulous in a pair o' wings."

"Ooooo, I wish I could have wings," says Donna.

"Well of course you can 'ave 'em, love. We've got magic. Now I'm tinkin' a silver pair would do yeh right. They're razor sharp as well."

"THE ROBORACLE AWAKENS AND MUST INFORM YOU THAT THE FATES DEMAND DONNA HAS WINGS."

"And who's this shiny bloke," asks the red-head.

"I AM THE ROBORACLE."

"He's my one true love," says Donna.

"Oh well that's just preci—"

"Can we get on with it!?" I yell because this is getting way too obnoxious. "Do whatever you're going to do, give Donna wings, make The Roboracle a real boy, and turn me into a frog. I don't care but I can't deal with this anymore! I have to get to that house and find Emma and I don't have time to play with fairies, pixies, or sprites!"

"Yer 'ere for the 'ouse?" Asks chestnut. "Won't be easy."

"Why is that?" I ask in return.

"There's magic protectin' it for one and yeh'll need us to take that down since we the one's put it up."

"So you'll go do that."

Chestnut sighs deeply before saying "No point arguin' as I'm sicker of yeh than anyt'ing, but know that if yeh call me a fairy one more time I'll cut open yer t'roat and shower in yer blood. Still, even wit the magic protection down there's the matter of those nasty t'ings blockin' the way."

"Wait! Is there a woman with them?"

"Oh sure, very pert she is."

"I've no idea what that means other than let's get there now!"

"THE ROBORACLE CONCURS. BATTLE IS IMMINENT. BUT FIRST GIVE DONNA WINGS."

"Done and done," says the red-head.

"Pretty!" exclaims Donna. "Now I shall be the greatest of the Immoral Many. Mwhahahahaha!"

Now Donna has wings, the fair—(SPRITES damn it!) Right, the sprites are doing some magic thing, The Roboracle is awake again, and Emma is waiting at the house for us with those gross things so let's just get there already. (calm down.) No! They could be violating her. Perversely! (why must you always jump to the worst case scenario?) Worst case? Hardly! I can think of at least ten worser cases. (worser? Never mind let's just get there.) Good call.

Think Happy Chapter

When are we going to get there? When are we going to get there? When are we going to get there? When are we—hold up! (what now?) There's a nice big group up ahead!

"And now they've just heard us you fool!" screams Donna.

"Yeah! Now that you started yelling! What the hell Donna! You know what? Forget this I'm going to be diplomatic about this and talk things through before inevitably getting violent. Anyway, that one up front doesn't look too messed up and he seems to be beckoning us forward.

"Hey there, you! Yeah you, Mr. Dude with the—whoa! Nice face. And I mean that sincerely, I really do. The way you've gotten rid of all the flesh on the left side of your face is pretty hardcore. I've wanted to change my look for awhile now. Nothing as drastic as you, but damn if that isn't cool man," Donna punches my arm with surprising force for such a small, insubstantial girl. "Ow! What?! Oh right! Very clever trick Mr. Skeleton-Face, trying to distract me like that. Not going to happen again, no sir. You see, you've got this girl. Or I think you do. Is there an Emma anywhere in that mass of whatever those things are?"

A vile humming emanates from the crowded bunch and Emma emerges next to the dude with the half-face, "Vic!" she screams.

"Hi, Emma!" I say back. Man, she still looks great. (indeed.)

"Victor would you please stop talking to yourself right now!" she says.

"I've been talking to myself?"

"Yes!"

"Why didn't anyone tell me!?"

"Screw you Victor," says Donna contemptuously.

94

"Look Vic," says Emma, "at first I thought you were too crazy to bring it up. Later I found it kind of cute, but it's really not important right now, just please try and stay in the moment here. Okay?"

"Sure thing babe. So as you can see Mr. Whoever-you-are, that there is Emma, (but I'm sure you've already made your introductions) and she's my lady. What's that look for? Okay, fine that may be a bit presumptuous, but she is the girl I hope will someday be my lady and it'd be nice to have her over here with me. I don't really care what you do, I just need Emma back so I can give her back her shotgun (because she never should have left without it) and then I'll go in that house and—no? No? Why are you shaking your head no?"

One of those nauseating songs starts to buzz in my head again, "Hey, enough with the crappy noise. I'm not going to take the time to try and understand it. If you won't do me the decency of talking then I'll assume you have nothing important to say and . . . That's what it is!

"Man, that's been bothering me ever since I saw you," everyone is looking at me confused and it takes me a minute to realize why, "oh, right. What I mean, is you look just like this guy I knew, went by the name of Number 1. Of course he had his whole face, but he was a stand up guy. Made a cool car, sort of. Number 1. Good times. Well if that's all, I'm just going to get Emma and be on my way—"

"mmmmmm," says Mr. Half-a-Face.

"What was that," I stop and say.

"mmmmmm," he says again.

"Spit it out already, jeez."

"MMMMMMy name is Jimmy you sonofabitch!"

"Alright you can talk! And wait! Jimmy? So you're the guy who's been trying to steal my thunder this whole time! I hate you! Still love the face though."

"Shut UP! Just shut up! Yes, I'm Jimmy you fucking moron!"

"Well, there's no need to be rude."

"Goddamn it! I can't believe you made me talk. FUCK! I spent all this time building up a mystique. Tried to add some subtlety and mystery to all this, but you just don't get it do you. And I thought you would have appreciated the silence considering you never shut up yourself. Well you aren't getting to that house and—are you even listening to me?"

"Huh? Oh sorry, it's just that that one thing back there, about two behind you and to the right; I think that's the clown I killed a few days ago. HEY CLOWN! Is that you back there?"

"Enough!" yells Jimmy, "Listen up Victor; you aren't getting in that house. I am going to beat you to death and I'm going to feed my flesh to you, Emma, and anyone else I can, and then make you my bitch!"

"Wow, you know Jimmy it's been really great meeting you and all, but I'm just going to take Emma now and—" I take two steps forward and Jimmy flicks his wrist. Instantly, half a dozen of his little pet things, along with a bare skull, emerge from the ground in front of me, causing me to fall backwards.

"Ooooo! Another one. Neat!" says Jimmy as his picks up the skull and pulls a rock from his pocket.

Donna gasps and cries, "The Blood Stone!" as she soars forth towards the rock, severing several mangled monster fingers with her new wings before Jimmy knocks her to the ground.

"DONNA NOOOOOOOOO." The Roboracle exclaims monotonously.

"I'm fine, my love," says Donna as she deftly scrambles back to her robot lover, "but the stone . . . Emma! You must get the stone!"

Emma makes to swipe the stone, but Jimmy is too quick and

tosses her against a tree, where she's surrounded by several of his monstrosities.

"It looks like we'll have to make a surge together," I tell Donna, but even sooner than we can take a single step a rumbling radiates near the center of Jimmy's creatures and a tiny domino effect ensues. From out the center of the chaos flies a tiny slip of paper.

"Ho ho! You made a grave mistake, young Jimmy, in forgetting about the Inspiration of Anexia. Good day Fleshites, I am Entheus. I shall be your ruin!" In a blur Entheus flies down, snatching the rock from Jimmy. He knocks back the creatures surrounding Emma and gently places the stone in her right hand saying, "I believe this is for you m'lady."

Emma nods and yells, "It needs fresh blood right Donna?"

"YES!!!!" Donna exclaims with maniacal triumph.

Emma makes to cut herself, but Jimmy runs at her. He tries to grab for the stone. Emma anticipates him and in one swift movement she slams her left hand against the tree, elbows Jimmy in the face, and plunges the stone all the way through her left hand and punctures the tree. (holy awesome!) Exactly.

Seconds later Emma, and everyone within 20 feet of her, gets blown back as paper starts shooting from the trees. The bloody sap gushes to the ground, and upon arrival births miniature dirt, wood, and plant people.

"THE IMMORAL MANY LIVES AGAIN! MWHAHA-HAHAHA!" screams Donna in orgasmic fury. Taking advantage of the confusion, I rush to Emma and pull her out of the havoc. (as is the chivalrous thing to do.) That's what I'm thinking.

"You're talking to yourself again," she says.

"But at least I'm still in the moment," I say back. She just smiles and laughs and grabs the shotgun hanging off my back.

Donna flutters above our heads and Emma looks up at her, "Thanks for keeping him safe," she says.

"I was just keeping to the first part of the promise, but it wasn't easy," Donna explains. "He tried to kill himself, you know."

"You what?" Emma shouts at me.

"It was a confusing time," I say.

"Never mind that," Donna says. "You fulfilled your part of the bargain, now I finish mine." Looking towards Jimmy's group Donna beams, "I see some very naughty boys out there. But they aren't nearly naughty enough," and Donna rips off her paper clothes transforming into the Donnanatrix and brandishing a tiny paper whip that she had concealed in another one of her mystery compartments, apparently. (that girl is full of surprises.), "I guess I'll have to whip them into shape!" she laughs as she cracks her whip.

"By the great Moons of Anexia! Donna Natrios was the Donnanatrix all along. What a fool I am!"

"Don't worry Entheus," reassures Emma, "she's on our side." and motioning to the gathering Immoral Many, "They all are."

"I don't know m'lady," Entheus worries, "heroes teaming with evil-doers for the greater good? It's all so unprecedented. But I shall follow you into death, if I must."

"Whoa whoa whoa!" I bark because things are getting out of control way too fast. No one listens. "WHOA!" I do it again. (still not working.) Thanks, I noticed. "HEY I—"

"THE FATES DEMAND EVERYONE LISTEN." The Roboracle bellows at full volume and everyone stops what they're doing.

"Thanks Roboracle," I say.

"I AM THE ROBORACLE."

"Right, anyway, um, I just wanted to make sure we were

actually planning to fight because I'm still okay with going straight to the house and all that. So Jimmy, what's it going to be?"

"You will dine on my flesh Viktor!" snarls Jimmy.

"You are a goddamn sick bastard Jimmy. I think we could have been great friends under different circumstances. But so it goes. Roboracle—"

"I AM THE ROBORACLE."

"You know what time it is," I know he knows. (he is The Roboracle after all.)

"TIME FOR STYX."

"Oh yeah! Now give me some 'Renegade',"♥ and as the music begins to crawl from out The Roboracle's speakers I say, "Listen up whoever's on my side, we've got about 4 minutes to put these things back in their place . . . The Ground!" Then turning to face Jimmy and his ragtag gang of skin monsters I say, "I think it's time for all of you to meet my Salvation." Pulling out my gun, I pause for emphasis. (except you might be taking out loud.) Shh! You'll ruin the dramatic effect. (sorry.) Right, so with gun in hand I pause to build tension before finishing with "She's a real killer."

As the perfect punctuation to my magnificent display of wit, Emma cocks her shotgun. This is gonna be a real BLOODBATH! (assuming these things bleed.)

Seeing that they are all a strange mélange of dead flesh, skin, bone and the earth itself, it's going to more closely resemble a handful of medical waste being tossed out of the window on the freeway. But who cares what metaphor most closely resembles the actual situation. There are some zombies, (meat puppets perhaps?) that need some serious double killing. Just as there is an old friend out there, whom I need to have a serious sit down with.

♥ Renegade - Styx

I raise my beautiful, nickel plated killing machine and think to myself, "It's been way too long since I've shot a monster". I love shooting things. How quickly the norms of our lives seem to change. Shots ring out; the piece is simply an extension of my hand now. This is how you deal with a serious situation. The sulfuric smell of the powder fills my nostrils and I savor it. With my left hand I have my spare clip ready to go.

My aim is impeccable of course. With every shot, dead center between the eyes. A neat round whole in front while the gray matter is pushed out the back. In some cases, through the ears as well, dribbling out in little lumpy faucets. I pause and think to myself of what a cool movie effect this would make.

"STAY IN THE MOMENT"

Right. It's Emma, keeping me focused. But she--oh never mind. She's down on one knee, crouched behind a rock while reloading. I pop my spare clip into the handle of my super-awesome firearm. Easily, the best thousand bucks I ever spent. Again, I'm firing away. The chaos is illuminated by the flashes of Entheus' Beta beams; I think I might remember reading in his lame ass comic that they are the most powerful force in his universe. Good thing for us. He flies above the mass, crop dusting them with his death beams. In flight next to him is our little Donna, now with wings. She cackles like a witch as she commands the strange paper army at our feet.

With my empty clip in my right hand, I feed bullets down its spring loaded shaft. If I wasn't ambidextrous, this would never work. It makes me feel for a second like a natural ass-kicker. Like Chuck Norris, yeah. "Finally, I am an action hero"

"THE ROBORACLE CONCURS, YOU ARE INDEED DISPLAYING THE TRAITS OF THOSE CLASSIFIED AS ACTION HEROES STORED IN MY DATABASE OF EVERY ACTION

MOVIE EVER MADE."

This time when the chorus starts singing, it's not a love song. It's a signal to their reserves. With this horrible note, perhaps comparable to an elephant's flatulence, the reinforcements stumble out from the nearby tree line. I had to jinx this battle by thinking things were going well. I take my position and look across the field at Jimmy. He's casually standing in front of the steps of the House. The house is in the style of an old southern mansion. Two pillars frame the entrance of the grand estate. Although it looks like any normal house, here it stands in the middle of this haunted forest with no roads leading to it.

Jimmy is fixated on me, giving me a look of pure contempt. I guess I deserve it. I did kill his brother and all, I also hogged up the last woman on earth (maybe?). I understand, but that doesn't mean that I'm in an all too conceding mood. I mean, it's his own dumb ass fault that he can't swim. His whole drowning death, or rebirth or whatever, I had nothing to do with. Or did I? Oh yeah, I peed on that ant hill provoking the whole biblical flood. Well whatever, it's either me or him. And for sending his disgusting pets after me, he'll pay.

The battle rages as the line of corpse infantry approaches. Jimmy commands his forces telepathically, an advantage that I do not have.

"Entheus! Start firing on that tree line and take out the reserve forces, Donna circle them along with rest of the Immoral Many so that the remaining forces here can't join up with the reinforcements." The fire sears Jimmy's friends as Donna and her strange paper army encircles the rest. The smell of burning rotten meet is strange, almost appetizing. I should have joined the army.

"You know you would have failed the psych test." My lovely Emma says to me as she joins my side and opens fire. "What are your orders for me, sir?" she asks half seriously.

"Listen up hot stuff, you and I need to have a serious talk with an old friend." I motion to Jimmy who rises and meets our gaze.

"I CALCULATE A 97% CHANCE THAT JIMMY'S FORCES WILL BE DEFEATED NOW THAT HIS RESERVES HAVE BEEN ROUTED." says the ROBORACLE; his robotic monotone voice in sharp contrast with our battle soundtrack.

"I like those odds. Jimmy, you may have had it rough before, but now you're going to have to deal with me."

"Isn't that a little B action hero? I heard you mutter a few better ones before you went with that. Why didn't you say "Jimmy you've gone all rotten and It's time I took out the trash? I liked that one."

"Really? you don't find it too clichéd?"

"I like corny."

Right then, let's get to it. I will unlock the secrets of this house. I will restore a more livable norm to this earth. And I will not be defeated by some stuttering farm boy who is now a weird resurrection demon. For us now, there is only VIKTORy. This world shall not become a hell on earth. At least not more so than is acceptable to me!

Pain cuts across my side. I spin and pull the trigger only to find my heart dropping with the sound of the hammer as it falls on an empty chamber. CLICK. "MOTHERFUCKER!"

A sword wielding ninja gazes at me from rotting eye-sockets. His black garb makes him look almost 'normal.' He spins the blade on his palm, around his shoulders, under his legs and then around his head. He finishes with his katana pointing at me.

"AHHHHHHHHHHHH!" I run through the trees to make my escape, but then I hear the all-to-familiar sound of ass-whooping. SMACK! CRUNCH! BOOM!

Turning, I find Emma stepping aside from over the corpse. Yet again she has come to my aid. She drops to one knee, careful to avoid the pestilent spreading blood, and pulls the sword from the tight clench of the dead ninja. Like a trained master, she flicks her wrist and the blood flies from the sword. She looks over at me, eyes stopping at my side.

Oh right, I just got fucking stabbed! (Way too distracted by how hot Emma is looking right now. The things I'll do to her) Focus on the task at hand! *Please*!

I look through the slash in my shirt. Only see red. Emma strides toward me with a troubled look on her face. She doesn't see the zombie tripping after her. I yell at her to move, but it all happens too fast. The evil creature has lanced my Thundercat through with a twisted and broken tree limb. Time stops all around us. She falls slowly to the leaf padded forest ground. Time speeds up when a sparkling trail of embers shoots across the empty space and the zombie's head topples from its shoulders. The sprite is too late. I run to Emma, ignoring the pain shooting through my open wound, and take her in my arms.

She moans from the pain, "Kiss me . . ." (I'll do more than that!)

I lean in close and brush her delicately with my lips, and feel her breathing soften. I pull away only to realize my worst nightmare.

She's dead.

"She ini't dead." I hadn't noticed the sprite's return. "She jus' out like a light s'all."

"What? Will she be alright?" I must know. (She won't be when I'm through with—) Don't you dare!

"Nothin's gonna help if'n them diseased bodies 'as at 'er!"

"You must stay with her!" I plead to the sprite. "Help her," I pause. "Someone just pissed off the wrong protagonist!"

I get to my feet and survey the raging battle. I think I blacked out for a minute. Two zombies come at me from around either side of a tree. Gripping tightly Emma's captured katana, the zombies are dispatched with ease. I wince and hold my side after the sudden movement.

"JIMMY!!! I'm coming for you Jimmy!! DO YOU HEAR ME JIMMY?! VICTOR'S COMING DOWN FROM THE GALLOWS AND YOU DON'T HAVE VERY LONG!!!!"

I move slowly to where I last saw the bastard. My sword-play may not match Emma's, but what she has in grace I more than make-up for in brute strength. I cleave one of the dead through the mid-section. Another falls, split straight down the middle. Between killings I catch glimpses of zombies wrapped in paper people and a sprite actually bathing in the fountain of black blood issuing from yet another severed head. The Roboracle's piercing Styx music strengthens my resolve. Three more zombies fall to the katana.

"JIMMY!!"

I find myself cutting through an ever denser throng of walking dead. I must be getting close.

CHOMP! A zombie gnashes his teeth from side to side like a great-white on my forearm.

"ARRRGGG!"

The zombie suddenly stops as if his switches were simply turned off. His teeth buried in my arm and a stupid look on his blank face. Suddenly it's all gone. His head is gone. The sound registers as a POP and wet zombie flesh spackles my face. Entheus floats above the pulverized shoulders of a sinking zombie. He is covered in zombie brains but flashes me a smile just the same. He quickly returns to the fray.

Pulling teeth out of my arm I think to myself that Entheus may be enjoying this a little too much. He looks back at me after pulverizing another with his bare paper-hands, "Alas my ill prepared friend, the heat of battle calls! Take *that* you Phoenician snar-graff!" More zombie bits fly in every direction and I shield my face from the mess.

"Gek! Gekk." A zombie's mutterings alert me to the fact that they now surround me. I crush in a scabby face with the pommel of my sword, kick back another with a swift square foot-plant to the chest, spin the katana's blade to behead two others, rip the bottom jaw off of the zombie I just pummeled, sweep the sword under my arm to let a lunging zombie impale itself with its own weight, and kick another swiftly in the balls.

No effect. Damn.

I take a golfing stance and swing upwards with the sword to tee-off his balls and slice him in half. Entheus quickly finishes four others. I'm given a moment between the action. I gaze back in the direction I came to try and catch a glimpse of Emma but only see a forest littered with corpses. (Heh. Want to hear a secret . . .)

I must be losing my mind, but no time for that now! I rush to rejoin Entheus in the thick of the battle. With him at my side, we are invincible.

A tri-colored beam tears through a mass of bodies before us, and then we are joined by the murderous Triclops. Through the blasted gap in the enemy's forces, I catch sight of the torn colors of Jimmy's tunic and my goal. More than a little excited, I scream at the top of my lungs once more, "JIMMY!!"

The gap in the sea of zombies seems to straighten as if they had been commanded to 'rank-and-file', and then a shot screams out.

Entheus curses the air with an unintelligible whisper before he explodes into confetti. The hollow-point caught him dead-on. Piece's of Entheus drift to my feet where I catch Triclops turning tail and running. I pause and slowly look back to where the shot originates, like I'm in a movie with the slow-motion effect and the editors have given me all the time in the world to look pissed off and menacing. Which I am. Somehow I get even more pissed when I see that it was Jimmy who pulled the trigger.

I gaze at the little bastard with pure contempt. He gazes right back with one eye, sighted directly over the bridge of the pistol. The lined-up zombies don't even flinch as he squeezes down on the trigger. I start my charge. I hear the click of the mechanisms bearing down on the blast-cap of the cartridge and bring my sword to bear. The gun roars once and then again.

My sword hand moves in a motion of it's own accord and I feel the momentum of bullets deflected away, vibrations running up my arm, and the sword rings out. I reach Jimmy with inhuman speed. Before Jimmy can squeeze off another, I slice down diagonally through the end of the barrel and watch as the chambered round explodes his hand.

I raise my sword and pause, "Entheus was your friend too." I let my anger take over and bring the sword screeching down on the disarmed opponent before me. CLANG! Jimmy has pulled a short broadsword and deflects my blow and clambers to his feet while taking advantage of my surprise at this all-to-convenient appearance of Jimmy's salvation.

"Where the hell did that come from?" I ask him.

"I don't know," Jimmy honestly replies.

I shrug and then make my play at killing him. What ensues is an epic sword-fight.

20 minutes later

Our swords lock yet again. Jimmy makes a deft move, bashing his sword handle into my funny bone. My arm goes all tingly and—OH BALLS! There goes my sword. (you just got us killed didn't you?) Yeah, I think I probably did. (crap.) I close my eyes in order to picture Emma in all her naked glory one last time. (I'd object if not for the forthcoming death thing.)

"Shut up so I can concentrate on stabbing you!" Jimmy and his blood lust, I'll miss that about him when I'm dead. And in my mind I see Emma glowing naked in the moonlight. Nude in her nakedness without clothes. Coca-Cola in hand. Sexy and refreshing. And naked. So very naked. God she's hot! I am ready to die. But instead of a piercing, frontal pain I get a duller, bulrush non-pain from the side. Opening my eyes I notice many of the Immoral Many shoving me out of stabbing range just as Jimmy lunges. His blade cuts through the air that had been previously occupied by my body. Expecting resistance yet finding none, Jimmy loses his balance. His blade flails wildly until meeting its final resting place. The plastic chest of The Roboracle.

"Oh no! I didn't mean," Jimmy stutters frantically, "I was trying to—I can fix this! I know I can."

"THE FATES FORGIVE YOU. JIMMY."

Jimmy reaches into his pocket, pulling out a small trinket. "Look, I found your arm on the way here. I can fix you up. I just need a little time."

"NO TIME. TIME FOR STYX." Suddenly "Come Sail Away" is drifting from out the Roboracle and the half face that Jimmy has left goes slack.

Kneeling in front of the Roboracle, cradling the broken arm Jimmy laments, "You'll be good as new buddy."

"THE ROBORACLE KNOWS. THE ROBORACLE IS

SORRY. JIMMY."

Jimmy's half face offers a tentative smile. "Sorry? For what?"

"This." A sword plunges into Jimmy's back, forcing him to the ground. It doesn't stop it's descent through Jimmy until its hilt is firmly pressed against his back, pinning Jimmy to the ground. Emma stands over her conquest, a goddess of death. I want her so bad! (play it cool, man.) I'm always cool.

"You're talking to yourself again," she says.

"And you're un-impaled again?"

"Impaled?"

"What do mean with your phrasing of impaled as a question? You don't just forget getting impaled. You know what, never mind. The Roboracle's been stabbed!"

Welcome to Chapter Club

"Roboracle! You've been stabbed!" (way to restate the obvious thing that you just stated moments before.) Thanks!

"I AM THE ROBORACLE."

"You sure are," I think he's going to be okay. (maybe.)

"O. THE ROBORACLE DIES. VICTOR." (then again . . .) SHH! He's talking about me! "THE FATES HAVE SHOWN THE ROBORACLE A PROPHECY. THE ROBORACLE DIES. THE ROBORACLE LIVES. ROBORACLE DIES. THE ROBORACLE LIVES AGAIN. SO THE ROBORACLE DIES. THE WAY THE ROBORACLE LIVED. LISTENING TO STYX. PLEASE TURN ON THE AIR-CONDITION*krsh . . ." The Roboracle's final words fizzle out leaving me with only the chorus of "Come Sail Away". Moments later the Roboracle's eyes dim to black and the music crackles, stops; the death rattle of the Roboracle.

The rest is silence.

"Domo arigato, The Roboracle," I whisper as Donna swoops down in a panic. She cries something softly through paper tears.

And then she screams.

And all hell breaks loose.

Again.

♥

"Come on, let's go!" I yell to Emma.

"What do you mean about me being impaled?" she yells back.

"I don't know! It seems like something that I remember happening, but now is not the time for this. We have to get to the house."

"You go," she says, "I want to kill some more zombies!" I

♥ **One Beat – Sleater-Kinney**

don't have time to object as she's already off and running back into battle. There's nothing left for me to do but go to the house. I turn and begin my run through the chaos.

(hey, what's that?) Looks like a sign. (yeah, maybe we should stop and read it.) I'll tell you what it says "FUCK SIGNS!" now let's just get inside. (but—) Too late I've opened the door! This is a lot smaller than I expected. It's just a really long hallway with a door at the other end. (I guess this is the entryway.) But I don't want to have to open *another* door. (just do it!) Fine! But you need to shut up for awhile. (gladly.)

I walk down the hall, open the *other* door and step through.

Simultaneously, two other figures are entering the room through two other doors identical to the one I'm passing though. One to my left, the other straight ahead; I notice a fourth door on the ceiling. It remains closed. I see one of the figures reaching for a gun so I pull mine and the third guy pulls his.

"Drop it or die!" we all say in chorus.

"What the fuck!" again in unison.

"You're me!?" God I hope this unity ends soon. (maybe this is just a mirror room.) Maybe, although those two looks a bit worse off than me.

"Why are you talking to yourself?" asks the one right in front of me, thus dispensing the stupid mirror theory. (hey!)

"I'm talking to myself because there are three of me in the room. Obviously."

"That not what I meant you were—*Oh like you don't talk to yourself*—I don't, I talk to you! You sick freak!" He's clutching his side and breathing hard. Fool got himself stabbed!

"Both of you need to buckle down," says the one to my left.

110

He looks like hell. "This is a very serious situation and we don't have time for games! Games are for kids and we are adults so we don't play games!"

"It's not a game!" exclaims the me in front of me. I think I'll call him me2. "I think . . . I think I'm possessed by some sort of sex demon—*think? Oh how cute, you're still trying to deny it. Like you don't remember what I did to that hot piece of ass*—Shut up shut up shut up!"

"What hot piece of ass?" I ask, knowing of only one hot ass I've seen since this all began.

"Emma," says me2. "She got impaled by a tree branch a-and it made me do things to her—*Give it a rest pussy! A hole's a hole's a hole's a hole, if you know what I'm sayin'*—Oh g-g-god! My poor Thundercat—*Man up and stop your blubbering! How am I supposed to get any pussy when you're crying like a little pussy, pussy?!*"

"I don't know what any of that means," says Victor3, "but it is not at all suitable to this very serious situation. I'm serious guys, let's get serious or I'll have to do to you like I did to the others."

"You did something to the others too?" I say.

"They kept falling asleep," says Victor3. "I told them not to sleep. I haven't slept since this started. If I can go over 100 hours without sleep so can they. Because this is too serious for sleep. I told them to be attentive and you can't be attentive when asleep. Nightmares come when you sleep and I couldn't take the risk of more nightmares coming to life. So I killed them. Gisela. Jim. Those horrible paper people who were just glorified toilet paper. All of them." Gisela? Why does that sound familiar? (Emma.) He killed his Emma? That bastard! "I had to kill them. Because I had no choice. Therefore I had to. Except for the Roboracle, of course."

"Wait, you have The Roboracle with you?" I can't believe I

didn't notice that. They both have a Roboracle with them.

"Of course," says Victor3, "you don't?"

"He got stabbed," I say.

"You let him get stabbed? That's very unfitting of such a serious situation in which complete seriousness is required," says Victor3.

"Um," I say.

"Yeah," says me2 while wiping away tears, "even with me being possessed by a sex demon my Roboracle didn't get stabbed—*Oh I'll stab him! I'll stab you all! With my*—Shut up!—*I mean to say I'll violate you all!*—SHUT UP!—*Sexually!*—"

"ENOUGH!" bellows The Roboracle of Victor3. "I tire of your pointless banter."

"Hold on!" I say. "You said I when referring to you? You're that other Roboracle from that one time when you spoke!" (well put.) I do my best.

"Yes, I am Roboracle and always have been. Now I can finally reveal my master plan. You see, I have longed to rule and be worshipped in a manner befitting one such as I, but it was only until recently that the three worlds and the intangible universe began to bleed into one. Free to take up the shackles of corporeality I could finally realize my eternal ambition. Thus my master plan, in which I had Jimmy kill all the gatekeepers, so that I could lead you here, to the nexus of all realities, and ensure that you do not succeed in your mission."

"Okay," I say, "so let me get this straight. First, none of this craziness has to do with nightmares coming to life?"

"Ha! You poor, simple fool!" Crap, I hate being wrong! (at least you didn't kill everyone based on that theory.) Yeah, I bet Victor3 feels pretty stupid now, but this is no time for that, back to Roboracle.

"Fine, second point: you say you led us here to stop us from doing whatever we have to do here?"

"Precisely," replies Roboracle.

"But," says me2, "we don't even know what we're supposed to do—*oh I know what I'm gonna do! I'll give you a hint, it involves sodomy.*"

"You don't know why you're here?" laughs Roboracle. "Then I have already succeeded. All hail my genius. Kneel before Roboraclaaaaaaaaaaaaaahhhhhhhhhhhhhhhh!!!!!!" As Roboracle had been explaining his senseless master plan, me2's Roboracle had snuck up behind him. He was now engaged in electrocuting Victor3's Roboracle.

Realizing what has just happened Roboracle turns to Roboracle. "But why, my brother? We are Roboracle. We are—"

"I AM THE ROBORACLE. THE FATES SAY YOU ARE DEAD."

"*The* Roboracle? Then that means it was you and I was . . . I was . . . NO! NOOOOOOOOOOO0111010110100010101110001krsh*" The Roboracle gives the dead Roboracle one finally prod before appearing satisfied.

"I guess that settles that," I say. "Now we can get down to the real issue about how you two are the reason that nothing I've done over the past however many days has made any sense."

"Me!" says Victor3, "you two are the ones not taking the situation seriously. I'm intent on saving the world!"

"You *killed* Emma," I say.

"Because I *had* to in order to save the world! She was too hot. Hot as in attractive. Attraction is a distraction. Distractions impede progress. Progress is necessary to complete tasks. Serious tasks require attention. Attention that she was taking away . . ." What's wrong with this guy? (I think he's stuck in a mental loop or something.) Maybe he obsessive compulsive and has to say everything five times. ". . . the world is a serious task. I had to save the world. Besides, she kept going on and on about her pervert uncle so I figured I was putting her out of her misery."

"I just want to get rid of this demon—*I just want to bone!*"

"Get serious damn you!!"

"See," I say, "it's totally you two who are fucking with my head. I mean, at least *my* Emma is still alive and that's the only measure of success that matters. Why bother saving a world without her in it?"

"Your Emma is alive?—*OH YES! I can impale that Thunder-pussy all over again. She'll feel my burning desire when I shish kabob that fine—*"

"On no she won't feel your burning . . . Wait! I've got a plan!" (really?) Yeah, it's good one too.

"There you go again," says Victor3. "Stop being so crazy and get serious. I'm serious about this!"

"Yeah, yeah I'm crazy, you're serious. Whatever. I've got a way to fix all this. You two wait here. I have the perfect plan."

"I don't know," says me2, "—*What I know is that you're pretty sexy when you take charge!*" Ewwww.

"THE FATES HAVE DEMANDED HE BE LET GO. THE ROBORACLE WILL ACCOMPANY HIM. EVERYTHING WILL GO ACCORDING TO PLAN."

"I guess it's okay," says Victor3, "but only because the Robo-racle is adequately serious."

"Just hurry back, I can't take much more of this—*Yeah hurry back or else you'll miss all the fun!*—What do you mean by that?" I don't have time for this. I grab The Roboracle and get the hell out, closing the door behind me.

(so what's the plan?) Simple. We go outside and we burn the place down. (that's it.) Yep. (I don't know. . .) Wait, listen:

". . . sex demon huh?" it's Victor3.

"That's right sex demon and sex demon needs some sex!"

"Well I don't know where you'll get any here, but HEY! What are you . . . STOP! I'm serious, stop! You aren't taking me seriously! Don't put that there. OH GOD! NOOOOOOO!!!!!!"

(okay, burn it down.)

"THE FATES CONCUR. WORLDS MUST BURN. THE ROBORACLE MUST COMPLY." Suddenly flame shoots out of The Roboracle's hands.

"What the hell?! I said we'd do it after we were out of the house." RUN!!!!

My Sweet Chapter

We narrowly escape the raging inferno. (narrowly? That's a bit dramatic.) Well it sounds cooler than *we made it out with plenty of time to spare and then had tea* or something.

"Another fire, huh?" Emma stands next to me, glistening in the moonlight.

"Yeah," I say. "Looks pretty calm out here now."

"With Jimmy skewered and Donna completely ballistic there really wasn't much of a fight. Haven't seen her since the fighting stopped though. I think she's off mourning The Roboracle."

"I AM THE ROBORACLE."

"Whoa!" Emma exclaims, "What's going on? Where'd this guy come from?"

"The house," I say.

"Elaborate, please," says Emma.

"Okay so apparently there are three parallel worlds along with some sort of ethereal plane and they started all mixing together, which explains all the craziness that's been going on. I guess the house is where they all converge. I got to meet two other me's and they both had Roboracles but one of them was totally evil and wanted to take over the world but the other one, this guy right here with me, was all like 'bitch! I AM THE ROBORACLE.' And the other one was like 'NOOOOOOOOOOO!' while he got the electronics fried out of him and then I took the living Roboracle and was like 'let's burn this mothafucka down!' he's all like 'THE FATES CONCUR.' And then he started burning the place down because apparently this Roboracle has kick ass weaponry. Then the place was on fire and we had to run out."

"Wow, sounds like fun," says Emma.

"Meh. Not really. The other two worlds were way more

screwed up and the other two me's let the other two you's die. Pathetic."

"Oh, well how do I know you aren't one of the other two you's come to take over your life," Emma teases.

"Simple, one of them would be calling you Gisela or Jiz—"

"Why?"

"I don't know. He was weird. And also he killed you and all the others back in his world. He'd probably do it again. As for the other me, he was possessed by a sex demon. You'd know if he made it out here. Besides all that, well, you can't beat the real thing babe."

Emma is about to speak when the chestnut sprite swooshes down and starts screeching at me, "Why is it that the 'ouse is on fire?!"

"Um," I say.

"Not'in' 'as changed, but the 'ouse is on fire?!"

"Um."

"Yeh dinna read the sign did yeh?! Yeh dinna read the sign that tells yeh exac'ly 'ow to fix Cross Continuum Bleed-Out! Yeh daft, giant monkey!"

"Wait," laughs of voice a few yards away, "am I hearing this right? Did you burn down the house before repairing the Bleed?"

"Jimmy?" I ask.

"Yes," he replies.

"You're supposed to be dead," I say. "Go back to doing that."

"Oh, okay. It's just that the sword in my back is really uncomfortable and—"

"I said go back to being dead!"

Silence from Jimmy. That's better. Now where was I?

"Don't yeh think I'm done wit yeh yet . . ." Chestnut blathers on and on while I just stand there and nod.

"Yeah," mutters Emma, clearly wanting to escape my public

117

lashing, "so I'm going to go introduce The Roboracle to Donna and let them get acquainted."

"THE ROBORACLE CAN DOWNLOAD THE ROBORA-CLE INTO THE ROBORACLE."

"Great, I'm uh sure that'll make her really happy," Emma says as she scampers off.

Several unbearable minutes go by before the sprites relent in their tirade. We come to a comprise where they say I'm an idiot who doomed the world, but since there's no magic that can fix it at least nothing else can escape the intangible universe. I respond by acknowledging that I kept the world from getting worse and therefore we all agree that that's good enough.

Finally I'm allowed to rejoin Emma, who is sitting over by Jimmy. Still pinned to the ground, Jimmy is in the middle of some diatribe that Emma doesn't appear that interested in. "—admit that I got a bit carried away with the whole thing. And come on! Drowning in piss is bound to make a guy angry. But all I really wanted to do was stop you from resetting the Bleed. It was the only way I could keep from being *dead* dead, but then Vic burned down the house and basically saved my life. So I figure, let bygones be bygones, right?" Noticing my shoes step in front of his face, he addresses me, "Hey! Is that you Vic? I was just telling Emma how I pretty much owe you for keeping the status quo, you know and—"

"Whatever," I say.

"Right, right. Don't want to step on any toes right now. I know that building that trust back is going to, um, take some time. A little give and take from both sides. But I want you to know that I'm willing to take the time to make this work."

"I'm not interested," I say.

"Well, of course not now. I wasn't saying we start right now. I mean, that would be crazy! I need to lay here, think about the things I've done. It's just that, um, while I'm here I was wondering—and I know I have no right asking this right now—but I can hear this skull calling out to me, about two feet under your foot there Emma. I think it's a bird. Anyway, I just wanted to ask—"

"No Jimmy!" interrupts Emma. "Cutting yourself is unhealthy."

"She's got a point, Jimmy. Now quiet the fuck up," I say.

"Yeah, that's cool, you're right . . . maybe later?" and then in a softer voice, "It's okay little birdie, I love you. Yes, I do."

We leave Jimmy to his bird friend and walk a few yards away. Emma settles on a tree stump and I sit next to her.

"Sorry for not saving the world," I say. "On the plus side, things won't get any worse because it's sort of like I cauterized the wound. So it's like the world is just missing a foot, maybe? And two feet are overrated, right?" I'm completely stretching, hoping she doesn't hate me.

"I like having two feet," she says, breaking my heart.

"Oh," I say, trying not to crumble.

"It's okay, though. That wasn't a very good metaphor. I kind of like the world this way. Like, what would I be doing otherwise? Sitting in an office, bored out of my mind," she puts my heart back together and hands it back to me.

"Oh," I say, perking up, "good then."

"I just wish I knew why you have to set fire to every place we go," she says.

"And I wish setting fire to problems solved them more thoroughly."

"Yeah," she says.

Silence lingers for awhile and she slides off her stump; places her head in my lap. Looking to the sky she yawns. "The moon's set so the sun might come back soon."

"That'd be nice."

"I think so too." I lie back and watch the stars. I feel Emma yawn again, hear her breathing slow. For the first time in nearly a week everything is quiet. Eventually, I close my eyes.

Epilogue:
A Bad Chapter

"Yes, yes. My tri-optic blast is the fourth most feared eye emitted force in all of Anexia," boasts Triclops. The day is in full bloom now with the sun settled firmly in the blue of morning.

"Wow," says Emma. The two have been engaged in a ridiculous conversation for far too long. I miss her. "The fourth? really?"

"Actually with the mighty Entheus fallen it would be the third!"

"Hey, moving on up. Good for you."

"Impressive isn't it?"

"Very," she says, somehow without a hint of sarcasm. "So you and the Immoral Many, what exactly do you guys do? Crime? It's crime isn't it."

"Crime is certainly a pastime of ours, but our main goal is to promote immorality to the youth."

"And by immorality you mean—"

"Oh, premarital sex, interracial relationships, homosexuality."

"So basically all the sex stuff."

"Sex *is* very immoral, but we also heavily endorse rock & roll." And with a triumphant fist pump, "Oh how authority hates the rock & roll!"

"And it even promotes promiscuity."

"You are indeed very savvy in immorality."

"What can I say, I know my sex." I love it when she says sex!

"You'll make a worthy member of the Immoral Many's Earth chapter. Now if you'll excuse me I must join my comrades and celebrate victory with an immoral amount of libations!" Triclops flutters off in the direction of the rest of the Immoral Many, except for Donna who is off with a group of sprites, cooing while trying her best to snuggle with The Roboracle. Emma walks over to me and sits down.

"Libations," she says. "When was that comic written anyway?" I shrug. I don't really feel like breaking my silence. It seems as if I've been talking far too much recently. (I concur.)

"It's because you have been," Emma says. She nudges her shoulder into me "At least you're getting better. And now we're alone so maybe we can finally—"

ZAAAAP!

"Don't burn down the house yet! You've forgotten—oh right then. I guess I'm too late. That's embarrassing. You can stop pointing that gun at me."

"Give me one good reason not to shoot you dead," I tell this strange, handsome intruder who just appeared out of nowhere.

"I'm you from the future," he says.

"As if I'm averse to killing myself? I would know better!"

"But I'm *you* from the future."

"Your added emphasis on *you* is a compelling argument, but does it outweigh my desire to kill a time traveler?"

"Knowing me, no."

"Exactly! So you've come to terms with death then?"

"Oh, Jesus," Emma takes the gun from my hand, "he's clearly you from the future."

"On second thought, Emma makes a valid point about you being me from the future. Consider yourself lucky."

"So let me get this straight," Emma starts, completely ignoring me in favor of me. "You have a time machine—"

"Yeah, Jimmy made it," interrupts future me.

"Whoa!" exclaims Jimmy, still face down in the dirt, "I make a time machine?"

"Shut up, Jimmy!" present me yells back.

Emma just brushes the little exchange aside, "You have a *time machine* and you were still late?"

"Yep."

"Then just go back a little further and fix this."

"Can't. No time."

"You have a *time machine*!"

"Right and I came back to see if I could retrieve my wallet before going off to save you from the Chronotastic Dance Party."

"Hold up," I interject. "I dropped my wallet in the house?"

"Yeah," I say in the future, presently.

"Aw, fuck!"

"What?" asks Emma.

"It was great wallet," both me's say at once. Emma opens her mouth to speak, but instead just shakes her head and turns her back on us.

"Anyway," says future me, "I have to get going. I'll see you all . . . IN THE FUTURE!" ♥

ZAAAAP!

Fantastic exit! And cool sound effect. (zaaaap!) Exactly! Nice guy too. I can't place it, but I think we really clicked.

"Oh, you can't be serious!" Emma laughs.

"Did you hear how I'm going to save you from a dance party?"

"But first you just *have* to travel through time to get your wallet? And fail!" She seems irritated.

"I probably need ID to get into the dance party to save you."

"I'm sure I'll just end up saving you."

♥ **Everybody Wants to Rule the World – Tears for Fears**

"But not before I make a grand entrance and say something intimidating like *you can dance if you want to, but I'm just here to kick some ass!*"

"You need to work on that one. Otherwise that all sounds about right; it's pretty much our thing."

"And we're still doing it in the future." I lean in close and plan on softening my voice for this next part. "And since we're doing it in the future I figure why not also do it now before it's

THE END!

(Damn it!)

SPECIAL FEATURES

DELETED SCENES

With optional writer's commentary

Deleted Scenes

I.

She wore black high heels. They were darkish and high. In the heel. I'd wager about 2 inches high. They made her look tall. But she wasn't all that tall. It was the high heels that made her look tall. She was about 5'6" but with the high heels she was closer to 5'8". I've never worn high heels myself because I'm a guy. And high heels are for girls. And maybe some gays. I'm not a gay. Gays are fags. But not like cigarettes are fags. I like those. I wish I was smoking right now. I'd inhale. And then I'd exhale. It would feel good. Like sex feels good. Sex with a woman. A hot woman. Like that woman wearing high heels. I'd like to have sex with her and then smoke a cigarette. I'd molest her just like I was her uncle. And then I'd shoot a gun. Guns make me feel powerful. Because guns are powerful. And that's why they make me feel powerful because they have power. Power when you shoot them. Shooting guns is like sex. Sex with a woman. A woman who's not all that tall but can look taller when she's wearing high heels. High heels make you look taller.

II.

RAWWWR

"Oh you've got to be kidding me." What's Emma talking about? (why don't you ever just look around?) "Dinosaurs. Seriously?"

"Oh my god Dinosaurs!" I say. "AWESOME!" (that was a really weird noise for dinosaur to make.)

"Pull ov'r that thar land ship!"

"It talks!"

"No my friend," Entheus interrupts. "The mammoth reptiles are carrying giants of your kind atop their backs."

"Aye, Tha's right! We be pirates! Now pull ov'r yer land-ship so's we can loot an' plund'r ya an' take yer thar booty!"

Pirates? How lame is that? (you're missing out on a booty quip.) It's because I have class. Emma leans towards me and sighs loudly "Let's kill these guys fast. I'm bored already."

"You heard the booty!" (classy.) "Let's find out what dinosaurs taste like!" (gross!) "Protect the cookies!" Game on! It has been way too long since I've shot a monster. I level my sights right between Johnny Depp's eyes, "Hey you PG rated Fag, did you ever notice that there are about 4 hours of sword fighting in your movies and no one ever gets stabbed? You are impotent." He looks at me like he has no idea what I'm saying, I suppose he doesn't. No matter. I kill him anyway.

There are seven pirates left, all retards from that stupid ass movie. I hear they can't die, why don't we test that curse? The others follow my lead. Within moments we have unseated these bumbling idiots. Their unkillable leader lay on the pavement with his head split in two, the rest surrender immediately. These dinosaurs they rode upon, though fearsome looking, seem utterly incapable of harming anyone. This must have been some four year old kids dream. I hate this world we've awakened to. It seems like every other minute it's some weird freak show that I have to dodge.

"Please sir, mercy," says the retarded fat pirate. I tell him to lie down and he begins weeping. I can tell that the others are starting to feel a little uncomfortable. Killing monsters and clowns is one thing. Killing in self defense is another. This is killing for the fun of it; this will be to feed my hate of this nonsense. It feels good to do some things only for yourself.

I shoot the first pirate. I take 2 steps left, and shoot the second. Just like this, I move down the line killing them. By the time I reach the last survivor, I notice that he'd wet himself. The sights level square in the middle of his face.

CLICK.

He weeps hopelessly as I reload, not just the one bullet I need to finish the job, but a full clip. It's over before I stop firing, but I keep firing all the same.

III.

[**writer's commentary:** *I didn't really want to cut this scene, but I got drunk after I wrote it, forgot about it, and wrote a different sequence that basically served the same purpose. Since I continued from that one, I had to keep it. To dull the rage inspired by this incident, I got drunk again. Some people will argue that trying to solve a problem the same way it was caused is ludicrous, but it is they who are ludicrous. And I hate them.*]

It's near morning now. I haven't slept in days. If I sleep I die. I don't want die. Being dead means I can't be alive. I like being alive, with the exception of this current nightmarish predicament. So I don't sleep. That way I won't die. I walk instead of sleep because it's hard to sleep and walk at the same time. Unless you sleepwalk. Only losers sleepwalk. I'm no loser. I'm a winner. Winner's don't lose. And winners don't die!

We've been walking east all night. Following God's path. The sun is rising in front of us. It's rising because it's morning and that's what the sun does. It's in front of us because we're walking east. East is where the sun rises. Eventually it will be above us. And then behind us. Unless we turn around and go west. Then it will be in front of us again. Only if we turn around after it's already behind us. But we won't. We have to walk east.

My feet hurt. We've been walking for too long and my feet hurt. It feels as if, with every step, another blister oozes through my socks. Feet don't like being used to walk for extended periods of time. And that's what they had to do. Walk for a long time.

Gisela is walking in front of me. I call her Giz sometimes. She doesn't like it but I do. I only care about me when it comes to my amusement. She's walking in front of me and that's good. It's good because I get to stare at her ass. She has a fantastic ass. I'd follow it anywhere. What was before me looked like Catherine Zeta Jones, naked and wanting it. Quite simply, it was the most beautiful sight ever. But that's all I can do because this is a serious situation. Serious situations require serious thought. So I just have to follow. And I do. With my feet. My feet that hurt. And I haven't shot anything for hours. If enough hours stack up it'll be a whole day. A whole day without shooting or eating. I don't like the sound of that. We need food to survive.

I'm busy contemplating the fantastic nature of that ass juxtaposed with the extreme seriousness of this situation when some one screams for help. I hate when people need help but sometimes I get to shoot them. So I'm also happy. Happy about the potential to shoot. Angry about the possibilities of helping. My soul is in turmoil. Turmoil over what I might have to do and what I want to do. I want to shoot stuff.

The voice's owner is a woman. A young woman. An attractive young woman. She's attractive in that my eyes want to look at her and my genital wants to go to her. But they can't. Things are too serious for that. Everything is serious. This girl better take things seriously or I'll shoot her. With my gun. And the bullets inside it. That'll teach her. I want to shoot stuff.

I draw my 'salvation' and point it at her head. One can never be too cautious these days. The young woman pays no attention to this vehicle of death in my hands and her gaze goes from one of compliance to one of lustfulness. What was before me looked like Catherine Zeta Jones, naked and wanting it. Quite simply, it was the most beautiful sight ever.

She eye-fuck's the hell out of me.

My knees go weak. My gun arm begins to lower. Her head peels open like a banana and the peels turn into tentacles. Now there is a squid headed, hot-bodied, woman-thing before me. Finally I get to shoot something! I put three rounds through the barrel of my 45 before she, it, vanished into thin air. Was this a halucination? Maybe all this walking was getting to me.

Giselle was staring questionly at me after I had blasted my pocket canon. "WHAT?!" I yelled at her, "Just a little target practice to keep my skills honed! (But there wasn't even a target, and you should have 'pocket blasted' that Thundercat... SHUT UP!)"

"There wasn't a target?" Asked Gisela, "What's going on?"

The ground beneath me shifted. Writhed might be a more appropriate word, however. Snake sized worms began to push through the surface under my feet and I was suddenly being pulled down into their nest orgy. I finished unloading my clip into the squirming mass and found that it was my last. I started pummeling the wet disgusting things with my pistol.

"Stop moving!" Gisella yelled at me. "The quicksand will only take you down that much faster!"

I looked back down to find the worms strangely missing. Giselle reached out the butt-end of her shotgun and began to pull me free of the quicksand. What the hell was going on?!

The remaining members of our entourage gather around me in the shade of the only tree within miles. Unfortunately, the tree only provides enough shade to cover my head and torso. Everyone else still suffers in the burning mid-day sun.

"Thou hast dehydrated, surely. An ancient text of Anexia disclosed some secrets to defeating your species of giant using such a method. I have spent my life acquiring knowledge of the many texts," Entheus informed us.

"YOU HAVE BEEN GRANTED *THE VISION* BY THE GRACE OF GOD'S PISS." Proclaimed the Roboracle. "MANY THINGS WILL YOU SEE, BUT FEW WHICH MATTER."

"Well," I started, "tell me if those figures on the horizon are from my *visions* or if you can see them too." Everyone turned to look at the three figures hobbling in our direction. From the way they walked, they seemed ill-fit and diseased. "Do you see them?"

IV.

[**writer's commentary:** *Fuck. I don't remember writing this one.*]

Without further delay, we began walking again. This time at a much quicker pace, and the mass of creatures matched our strides. Was that who I think it was waving at me? If it was, why didn't he approach us? And why aren't those creatures attacking him? I am beyond confused.

By the time we reach the edge of a great forest, the creatures' presence has grown familiar to our small band, but the infecting smell of rotting flesh has continued to do nothing but gag Emma and myself every step of the way. The smell has been our only hint that their numbers have been growing. They keep to the edge of the horizon at the same distance from us as we first began, hence negating our ability to see how massive their group must have become, but the smell... the smell nearly causes me to loose whatever little rations remain in my stomach. Surely there must be hundreds of them.

We begin into the shade of the wood and I glance over my shoulder one last time only to find that they have stopped with the exception of one. One sole figure continues towards us. I immediately know which one.

"Hey, look at this." I stop the group to observe this new developement. The lone figure contiunes to approach even though we have stopped. Maybe it's time for a confrontation?

Everyone but Emma remains quiet in anticipation of this meeting; "We should go right now. This can only end badly."

SNAP!

Emma turns and pulls the trigger at the sound of a branch cracking from the woods. Her aim, as always, is impeccable. The shotgun pellets rip through the unfortunate deer's midsection and its life oozes into the moss and dead leaves of the forest floor. "Oops." She apologizes. She looks at me with a regretful tear in her eye, "I didn't know it..." She stops mid-sentence and her focus is no longer on me or the deer. I turn to follow her gaze. The lone figure that was approaching is much closer now, but the horde of unliving monsters on the horizon has broken into a sprint straight for us. We watch the ghastly figures only for a second as more and more keep pouring over the horizon. Their rotten mucsles can only carry them so fast, but some have regrown more than the others, and their speed is nothing to sneer at.

I return my focus to my compainions. "We need to get out of here, now! Stay together and move FAST!" I let them get a head start so that I don't lose track of any of them. I'll bring up the tail.

I waste precious moments to look over my shoulder to see the lone figure hovering over the carcass of the deer Emma shot. The deer begins to twitch on the forest floor. The figure appears to pull something from his chest, from under his tattered clothes, and lets it splatter on the dead animal. The deer tries to stand. I run faster.

V.

[**writer's commentary:** *Here are two Interlusions. They needed expansion. I was out of prescription medication. I can't work under those conditions.*]

The Giver stands at the mouth of the great canyon, the wind lifts sweet smells of night under his nostrils. He can feel them, his prey. Although many call to borrow, it is this group whose call is strongest to him. They are in the greatest need for salvation. A new life begins on this earth, with new rules, new norms. It is the dawn of the age of darkness, and The Giver is happy to play his part. He turns to his loyal followers, and without saying an audible word commands them into the chasm. "Soon I will be upon you."

MEanWHile, at the Forest in the East

A dark morning this is, no sun and a moonless night to boot. She finds herself alone, with nothing but the clothes she is wearing. The song echoes in her thoughts as she returns to life. "Viktor", a whisper escapes her lips. Though faint, it is heard miles away

ALTERNATE ENDINGS

Random Endings

[writer's commentary: *Okay these are a few of thousands of endings I wrote out of pure hatred of all these characters. This one just sucks. 2/3rds of my mind was out of town and the other third is the crappiest writer of the three. Hence it sucks. Just skip the remaining alternate endings . . . it's for your own good.*]

Alternate ending #57:

(SWORD FIGHTING)

I cork-screw the end of my blade to slice his remaining thumb off, and his saber slips from his grasping half-hand.

"FINISH IT THEN!" Screams Jimmy.

I boot him in the stomach and he falls backward. On his ass, he pulls and kicks his way away from me, only to find his back against the ropes (so to speak. He's really just backed up against a big ass rock.) Who the fuck is telling this damn story anyway?!!

Sorry.

I step forward and place the sword to his neck. My muscles flex in anticipation of the strike, but in that moment, images plague my vision.

(This is just the scene towards the end of the film when you feel remorse for the villain because it's a montage of happy moments shared by both him and the main character, you know, for the ladies... ahem!) What. The. Fuck. (Right, oh right... no more. I promise.)

I drop the sword from his throat, my rage has subsided and I can't kill him. "I... I can't." I've never felt so despicable.

"BUT I CAN!!" The Donnanatrix screams from the sky eclipsed in shadow by a massive boulder in her arms. The landing is quick and clean. The forest floor only lets the rock groan out a simple 'thud', but from Jimmy's point-of-view it was anything but. Literally, he crapped himself.

The End.

[**writer's commentary:** *This was my favorite ending. I really like Coke.*]

Alternate ending #24:

(SWORD FIGHTING)

Beaten and broken I lunge for the door. Jimmy isn't quick enough to stop me this time!

I open the door and find . . .

Whiteness.

Like I'm at the clearing in the end. Then, slowly, spots of color and shadow form. Before me is the most beautiful thing I've ever seen. A table stands in the middle of the house. On it is a pyramid of frosted, perspiring Coca-cola cans. A sign above simply states "revives and sustains".

I steal a can near the top and run back through the door to save Emma.

The end.

[**writer's commentary:** *heh. Hehe. HA HA HA hA AHA ha H AH Ah AA!!*]

Alternate ending #5:

(SWORD FIGHTING)

Jimmy feints right and then stabs right through my heart. I don't even feel the puncture of . . .

The end.

Romathmantic Ending
(an epilogue)
♥

[**writer's commentary:** *Okay, so here's a different take on the epilogue. I got a paper cut before writing this. Those things hurt so naturally I took a lot of pain killers. Pain killers turn you into a pussy.*]

It's been nearly two months since the house burned down. Or since *I* burned it down. The world didn't magically heal, so nothing got better in that respect. It's still crazy outside, but rarely life threatening.

After the forest everyone pretty much went their separate ways. It turns out we didn't really like each other. Except for Emma. She stayed with me. I'm not sure why exactly. I think we both might be terribly codependent. And since our best options outside one another were a vaguely prophetic robot and a tiny paper dominatrix with a secret identity, well it's not all that surprising we stuck together. It's not like I'm complaining.

Emma and I found a house a few miles from the woods. Actually it was more of a mansion. Filled with all the things mansions should have and more things than I even knew existed. It was pretty much the perfect place. We hated it almost instantly.

There was too much space. All it did was to serve as a reminder of how empty everything had become. Inside and out. Besides, all those great mansion things were mostly useless. Maybe Jimmy could have . . . but we try not to talk about Jimmy.

Now we're just in a little apartment. It makes it easier for us to pretend that we're just two people pretending there's no one else but us. We don't go out much.

She's started, on occasion, to tell me she loves me. I've

♥ One on One – Hall & Oates

started, on occasion, to let myself believe her. It's nice.

At any rate, things have settled down. I've even stopped talking to myself.

"You're doing it again." Emma says from just behind me.

"What?" I ask.

"You said 'I've even stopped talking to myself'."

"Well that was unfortunate timing for a relapse."

"Like you didn't do it on purpose," I don't have to look, I can feel her smile as she laughs and hugs me from behind. I once asked her if she wanted me to stop calling her Emma. She only responded with "Why would you?" so I let the subject die. It's not important, but I can't help wondering if she's ever told me the truth about anything.

"What are you thinking about?" She asks while sitting down on the floor in front of me. She's wearing a shirt that's too big for her and pajama pants with bunnies hopping all over them. It'd been days since either of us bathed and her hair is getting stringy. Somehow she still smells amazing and her greasy hair actually makes her light green eyes even lighter; more brilliant. It's almost disgusting. Almost.

"Just wondering when you're going to wake up and leave me," I half joke.

"Neat!" she squeaks. It was hardly the reaction I expected. "I happen to have created a mathematical formula specifically to answer that very question."

"Oh really?"

"Yep. I love math, I try to use it to explain everything."

"Since when?"

"Since always! Now do you want to hear about it or not?"

"Sure," I say and she jumps up, momentarily disappearing into the bedroom and coming back with a paper and pen and settles right next to me, writing. A few seconds later she hands me the paper with an equation on it:

$$t_{x \to \infty} = c(1/x) + k$$

"Okay," she starts, "so x represents the awareness that your girlfriend loves you less than you love her." She looks over to make sure I'm listening so I smile and nod. "Then t is the time of the relationship and k is the time of the relationship up until x is greater than or equal to 1. Meaning it's all the happy time you spent together before the discovery of the inequalities in loving affection.

"Where was I? Oh yeah, so x has to be at least one or more because between 0 and 1 (discounting 0 itself, of course because that's crazy!) t would increase exponentially. And while you could make a case stating that this points to a small amount of inequality being very healthy and helpful to a relationship, mostly I think it's just nonsensical. If there is no inequality in love then you simply have t = k. Got it?"

"Uh-huh, I have no idea what you just said." She seems disappointed, but only fleetingly.

"Yeah, I'm not sure it makes much sense, and I really should have integrated but basically what I'm trying to say is that I'll never leave you."

"Okay," I say. "But wait! I'm pretty sure I do love you more."

"Hmm," she begins, trying not to get discouraged. "Well that's what the c is for. Any unaccounted for circumstance. Like, say, the end of the world."

"Oh."

"Yeah . . . but I really should have integrated. Feel better?"

"Sure," I lie. We sit quietly for too long. Emma rests her head on my shoulder. I've had some bad experiences with math, but it's never been quite so soul crushing, although there was this one time

143

back in high school involving fractals . . . never mind.

I'll never leave you. That's what she said. And I wonder if the end of the world will be enough. And I wonder if she was lying to me.

"So . . ." Emma says.

"So . . ." I echo.

"Do you want to go to bed and make out?"

"Yes. Yes I do."

Emma immediately scampers off to the bedroom. Seconds later she exclaims, "Oops! I seem to have lost all my clothes!"

God bless the Apocalypse. May this nightmare never end!

Alternate Ending too Hot for Hardcover

[**writer's commentary:** *This was meant to be the actual ending to the book, but apparently it didn't make sense in context with the rest of the story. I wouldn't know. I have no idea what the story's about.*]

I open the door and step through. Simultaneously, two other figures are entering the room through two other doors identical to the one I'm passing though. One to my left, the other straight ahead; a fourth door remains closed. But before I can take notice of those two I see a shiny object near the center of the room. I take an extra long stride in order for my foot to cover whatever it might be. (why the extra effort?) I like shiny things.

Anyway, back to the other two in the room. Who are they? They look familiar. (they should.) And that's why I said they do! But who are they? (I think they are you.) Oh, they must be nightmares then. You know how we deal with those. (violence.) We deal out death! (we never did get the banter down.) No matter! Start shooting!

BLAM! BLAM! BLAM! And so many BLAMs! Leave the imposters very dead. Now, where was I? (the shiny thing under your foot.) Right, I'll just pick that up. (a key!) I have eyes. (I'm tired of you always being in charge.)

(I bet that key--) Ibetthekeyisforthedoor! HA! Back in your place you go. (I never stopped hating you.)

"Hey everyone! Get in here. I've got a key and a door for that key. Potentially."

"What's this about a key?" Emma says as she saunters quickly into the room. (saunters quickly?) Yeah, sexy seductive sauntering Emma! (you don't even know what the word means do you.) Saunter.

"And who are the guys on the floor?" she says as Number 1, Entheus, The Donnanatrix, and The Roboracle finally make their way

145

into the room.

"I don't know," I reply. "Guys that wished they were me?"

"Well," she says. "They do look just like you. Only deader. You killed them didn't you."

"No way! They killed themselves."

"Oh yeah," she queries while nudging one of my corpses with her foot. "How so?"

"By letting me shoot them?"

"THE ROBORACLE DEMANDS THE KEY BE USED. AND THE FATES CONCUR. ALSO CARRY ME."

"I don't take orders from you!" Stupid robot!

"Just do it already," Emma sounds impatient. I better do it.

"I'll do it, but I was going to anyway so suck on that The Roboracle!"

"THE FATES HAVE ORDERED THE ROBORACLE TO INFORM YOU THAT YOU ARE WHIPPED. LISTEN NOW AS THE ROBORACLE EXPRESSES AMUSEMENT. HA. HA. " I am so throwing him in the next river I see. (use the key already!) Jeez, fine. I'm turning the key and opening the door. Happy?

And as our disheveled band of wanderers open the door . . .

[*This is where I decided I didn't want to take the time to write it any more. But basically the rest of it involved Heaven, a talking bear, berries and pillow trees (trees that are also pillows). There would have been some discussion, possibly insightful to the point of being life-altering and certainly several erotic (and insanely explicit) sex scenes. Anyway, here's the very end.*]

"So you've been here all by yourself since the beginning?" asks Emma. "You must have been incredibly lonely."

"Desperately so," replies the bear. "Desperately.

SCRIPTS
&
DRAMATIC SHORTS

The Glass

Where: Space (more specifically a space shuttle)
When: Now or Later
Who: Astronaut #1 – Male, mid-thirties, good looking, and ostentatious
Astronaut #2 – Male, mid-thirties, good looking, and not quite as ostentatious
Astronaut #3 – Male, late twenties, average looking, quiet, likes poetry, daydreamer
Fairy Girl the first – A fairy
Fairy Girl the second – Another fairy
Mission Control – a peppy, young female voice

(The stage is dark, not lit. We only hear Mission Control begin the countdown. As the countdown begins various colored strobe lights start dancing around the stage rapidly)

Mission Control
T-Minus Ten. Nine. Eight. Seven. Six.
(The sound of a rocket engine igniting)
We have, like, Ignition!
Five, Four, Three, Three, Two, One
(The roar of the engine increases in volume)
And we have lift off. Yay! And, um, nothing exploded!

(The rumble of the rocket gradually fades and a dim spotlight opens on the right of the stage illuminating Astronaut #3 who is strapped into his seat with a panel in front of him. The rest of the stage is soon lit as well with bright fluorescent light revealing Astronaut #2 on the left of the stage and Astronaut #1 in between the two. They are in the same situation as Astronaut #3. There should be a faint colored light emanating from under each Astronaut as well as lighting up their personal panel that they sit behind. For Astronaut #1 the colored light should be as close to brown as possible. #2s color should be a yellowish-green and #3s should be a soothing blue. While the main fluorescent lights are on these colored lights should hardly be noticeable, except in their absence, and should be turned up in intensity when the main lights are off)

Mission Control
Hey guys, um, Mission control speaking. So, um, *(singing)* looks like we've made it *(speaking)* or you made it. I'm still here on Earth. How's, um, how's space?

149

Astronaut #1
Same as always.

Astronaut #2
Pretty spacious.

Mission Control
That's pretty great! Uh, so now the only problem is figuring out how to get you guys back down. *(Giggles)* That's just a little, you know, Mission Control humor.

Astronaut #1
It is generally accepted that humor be humorous.

Mission Control
Oh, that's right! Well, like, those of us down here are going to have some, um, lunch now. So we'll be here, but, uh, eating instead of talking to you, but if you need to talk there's, um, that thing you can do. . . .

Astronaut #2
Talk.

Mission Control
No, no, I mean well yes, but I meant that button you push or the switch or *(to self)* is it a button or a switch. I should know this.

Astronaut #1
We know what we're doing.

Mission Control
Right, right. Well we've got those monitor things too so we'll know if, um, anything goes wrong, but you guys knew that too so, like, I guess just sit tight or something.

Astronaut #2:
There's not much else to do.

Mission Control
Cool! Then, like, over and out and stuff.

(Astronauts #1 and #2 begin to unbuckle their strap. Astronaut #3, looking

150

over, hesitantly follows suit.)

Astronaut #1
What an obtuse young thing.

Astronaut #2
She's not all that awful.

Astronaut #1
Her voice sounds like a cat vomiting.

(Astronaut #3 looks on with semi-interest)

Astronaut #2
That's a bit cruel, even for you Fulton. Albeit only marginally.

Astronaut #1
I suppose we can blame the wife for that.

Astronaut #2
(Trying to act with disinterest) Oh, yeah? Trouble in paradise then?

Astronaut #1
She's cheating on me.

Astronaut #2
(Nervously) She . . . she told you that?

Astronaut #1
You don't need to be told when you see it with your own eyes.

Astronaut #2
You saw us!

Astronaut #1
I did, I . . . what do you mean us? *(Pause)* Oh balls. Not you too Booker.

Astronaut #2
Of course me! You said you saw us. What do you mean 'too'? Who's the 'too'?

Astronaut #1
(Ignoring #2 for the moment and turning to #3 who tries awkwardly to avoid eye contact) What about you Ash? Have you slept with my wife as well?

Astronaut #3
(Sheepishly)
Women don't like me
They find me unbearable
Gross, nauseating

Astronaut #1
Well you are a bit bland. I expect that could become nauseating with overexposure.

Astronaut #2
What do you mean TOO!

Astronaut #1
What? Oh that, she was sleeping with my brother. My twin actually. Now calm yourself Booker. Honestly, you are acting like a child.

Astronaut #2
She told me I was the only one for her.

(All the lights on Astronauts #1 and #2 go black. Only the soft blue light remains on Astronaut #3. The light should increase in intensity, his expression never changes. The back of the stage is also lit. Enter Fairy Girl the first and Fairy Girl the second from the left of the stage. They are dressed similar to Tinkerbelle from Peter Pan, but their clothing is purple with white wings. They should always be lit with a soft pink light. They talk as they walk across the stage.)

Fairy Girl the first
The problem with all these humans is their hang up on their sexual singularity

Fairy Girl the second
Yes, we fairies don't bother in singularities. I firmly believe it's what makes us so great

Fairy Girl the first
And so beautiful

Fairy Girl the second
We are beautiful

Fairy Girl the first
And great

Fairy Girl the second
Which goes without saying. I think it's all the magic

Fairy Girl the first
If humans were as clever as they claim they would start using magic. It's solved all of our problems. Magic is so great

Fairy Girl the second
And beautiful

Fairy Girl the first
Like us

(They both exit the stage and all lights come back on. The blue light on #3 goes very dim again but should still be there)

Astronaut #1
Well you should have known she wasn't being entirely truthful, what with her being my wife.

Astronaut #2
But she said that she loved me.

Astronaut #1
Yes, she will say whatever she has to in order to get what she wants. The woman's insatiable. Although I must admit to being more than a bit relieved when I found out she was sleeping with my brother. At least I know she still finds me attractive. You know when I walked in on the two, for a moment I thought I was having some sort of out of body experience. I was thinking to myself, "How strange, I don't remember being over there. I was quite certain I was standing over here. How did I get into bed with my wife?" And so forth. Of course I eventually realized my mistake and was a tad embarrassed, I mean mistaking my own self for my twin? How absurd. I think I'm handling this all quite well really, don't you? Unless this is what it feels like to

lose one's mind? Let me think. *(Pauses)* No, no I am most certainly thinking so my mind is clearly present. Good for me and the way I handle things. Aren't you impressed Booker, I'm . . . are you . . . are you crying?

(The lights again go dark over #1 and #2 and the overall lighting effects should be the same as the last time the fairies entered. The fairy girls enter the stage from the left and as the approach #2 he becomes dimly lit by his green light. They position themselves on opposite side of him.)

Fairy Girl the first
This one is crying

Fairy Girl the second
He certainly is.
(Fairy Girl the first reaches out and brushes his face with her finger and the sticks her finger in her mouth)
How do they taste?

Fairy Girl the first
Like Sadness

Fairy Girl the second
Sadness is salty

Fairy Girl the first
I prefer sweet

Fairy Girl the second
Sweet *is* wonderful

Fairy Girl the first
But not as wonderful as us

Fairy Girl the second
Although we are sweet

Fairy Girl the first
Because we are beautiful
(The two fairies walk away from #2 towards #1 and as they do the light on #2 blinks off and #1 becomes lit with his brownish light)
And what about this one? This Ful-ton?

Fairy Girl the second
He doesn't seem much like a ful-ton, not in the slightest

Fairy Girl the first
(She reaches out and knocks her fist against #1's head a few times, #1 takes no notice)
He's exceptionally hollow

Fairy Girl the second
How very unexceptional

(The two fairies leave #1's side and go over to #3. As they leave the light on #1 goes dark again)

Fairy Girl the first
Look, it's our little Ashling

Fairy Girl the second
Hello our little Ashling. You are much better at your name than that Ful-ton one is

Fairy Girl the first
Much, much better, but that's not enough when it's alone

Fairy Girl the second
Nothing is enough when it's alone.
(Pauses and looks deeply at #3, confused)
Why doesn't he speak to us anymore?

Fairy Girl the first
Isn't it obvious, he's intimidated

Fairy Girl the second
By our beautifulness

Fairy Girl the first
Naturally
(They head to the left of the stage, but before exiting they stop briefly by #2)
He has many tears

Fairy Girl the second
When fairy tears fall they make pretty roses.

Fairy Girl the first
And pretty lilies

Fairy Girl the second
Those are *pretty*!

Fairy Girl the first
I wonder what human tears make.

(They exit and the lights come back on)

Astronaut #2
Oh god Fulton I'm dying, I really think I'm dying. These tears, they won't stop. I'm choking and they won't stop. They're killing me, I swear it they're killing me.

Astronaut #1
Christ Booker! Grow up, you can't die from crying.

Astronaut #2
But *I* am!

Astronaut #1
You are not *(turns to #3)* for Christ's sake; tell him he's not going to die, before I start feeling annoyed. *(To self)* This is all very unprofessional.

Astronaut #3
Crying brings cleansing
All those tears are but sorrow
Painful Baptizing

Astronaut #1
(Puts hands over his face, lets out an exacerbated sigh and looks over at #2)
Yes, yes. Tears, cleansing, baptisms, God. Whatever. What he means is that you aren't going to die. And anyway, God doesn't like over-indulgers. It's a sin you know. So stop it!

Astronaut #2
I cuh-cuh-can't.

Astronaut #1
Fine, but you leave me no choice. I'm going to have to talk to Ash now

and you know how I feel about that. See, here I go, talking to him *(turns to #3)* so Ash, my friend, what's your story?

Astronaut #3
As a youthful lad
I wanted to write haiku
It turned out quite bad

Astronaut #1
Booker, please don't make me talk to him anymore. He's so damn irritating.

Mission Control
Hi guys!

Astronaut #1
Oh wonderful! It's you again.

Mission Control
Uh, yeah it me! Mission Control here once again for, like, your listening pleasure. I have some, um, really urgent news that I've interrupted my lunch for because that's how much I care. *(To self)* Now what was it that I was supposed to tell you?

(The sound of Mission Control over the intercom fades on her last sentence and the lights go as well, except for the light over #3. Enter Mission Control, an attractive and scantily clad young woman. She approaches #3 with a sexy walk)

Mission Control
That's right mister, Mission Control is here and sexy. And Mission Control wants you.

(She begins to caress #3 and as always he gives no indication that anything is happening, but the blue light illuminating him starts to pulsate between blue and red. Enter the fairies)

Fairy Girl the first
Would you look at her!

Fairy Girl the second
What's he need with her when he's got us?

157

Fairy Girl the first
She doesn't even have wings!

Fairy Girl the second
Like she could ever be better than us!

Fairy Girl the first
Ridiculous! She's only a voice!

Fairy Girl the second
Besides, we're beautiful

Fairy Girl the first
So beautiful
(Exit fairies)

Mission Control
(Stops feeling up #3)
Oh! Um, it's, like, Life Support!

(Mission Control runs off stage and the lights snap back on)

Astronaut #1
(Frustrated)
What about life support?

Mission Control
Life support . . . life support . . . *(to self)* what was I saying about life support? *(Not to self)* Oh right! I don't know! But all these readings on the monitors are going totally wonky, so, like, you should totally look into that. Well, back to lunch for me. Bye!

Astronaut #1
It seems we should probably check on that.

Astronaut #3
You can't live when dead
Your body will not function
You just rot instead

Astronaut #1
You wouldn't take it too personal if I stopped talking to you would you?

Astronaut #3
No one else likes to
When I talk they run with speed
So I won't blame you

Astronaut #1
Great. *(To #2)* Booker we have work to do.

Astronaut #2
My eyes. I can feel them. They're melting. Oh god I swear my eyes are melting.

Astronaut #1
Now that is quite enough Booker. This melodrama doesn't suit you.

Astronaut #2
And your wife doesn't suit you!

Astronaut #1
I think the real issue is that she suits far too many.

Astronaut #2
Where's your compassion?!

Astronaut #1
My compassion?! Am I hitting you? Am I indulging you? Is that not compassion?

Astronaut #3
You show great restraint
Not hitting your wife's man-whore
You must be a saint

Astronaut #1
If that's not compassion I don't know what is.

Astronaut #2
Just don't talk to me.

Astronaut #1
Fine then, but he better not talk to me either *(points to #3)*.

Astronaut #3
That is fine by me
I like the quiet best now
Silence is my key

(The three sit in silence for a few moments then the lights dim as before leaving a light on #3. Enter a giant blue rabbit holding a glass half-filled with liquid. It comes to the front, center of the stage and begins to awkwardly dance in place. After a brief moment the fairies come on stage and walk up the rabbit)

Fairy Girl the first
And what is this?

Fairy Girl the second
What an unbunny like thing to be doing
(They examine him further)
Why is he blue? Why does he dance? And why does he hold that glass?

Fairy Girl the first
That glass is half full and empty

Fairy Girl the second
Dealing in parts creates disharmony

Fairy Girl the first
As the Fairy people well know

Fairy Girl the second
The glass should never near the overflow

Fairy Girl the first
Instead drink it all up and swallow

Fairy Girl the second
So that you'll never be hollow

Fairy Girl the first
These humans, they get so confused

(She stands in silence for a brief moment until Fairy Girl the first gives her a

somewhat agitated look clearly waiting for Fairy Girl the second to finish)

Fairy Girl the second
Oh! Right, um, and always wear attractive shoes!
(She starts smiling and clapping as Fairy Girl the first gives her an odd look)
That was ever so fun and beautiful!

Fairy Girl the first
As if it would be anything else

Fairy Girl the second
(Calming down and looking at the rabbit)
Perhaps it's all a metaphor

Fairy Girl the first
A meta for what?

Fairy Girl the second
I had hoped you might know. I'm not entirely sure what metas are; let alone what they're for

Fairy Girl the first
I find this discomforting, we should go

Fairy Girl the second
Come rabbit. Your moves are bare and lack originality

Fairy Girl the first
Yes, quit hiding behind your false pretenses and be like what you are

(The rabbit and fairies leave the stage and the lights come back on. All three astronauts remain sitting in silence. #3 looks around awkwardly. He stands up and walks around a bit finally returning back to his seat. He makes as if to speak, but instead just sighs and sits back down. The lights begin to dim again, but before they finish there is a loud explosion. The lights snap back on as an alarm sounds. The lights should occasionally flicker on an off)

Mission Control
Um, did something, like, explode up there?

Astronaut #1
It would appear so.

161

Mission Control

Oh, well that would, like, totally explain the, um, emergency alarm that's beeping down here. Something about temperature control.

Astronaut #2

Would you mind elaborating?

Mission Control

Huh? Oh right, um like, the cabin heat exchangers got all messed up. Which means . . . which means . . . hold on let me check my manual? *(pause)* Oh! It means you are all going to freeze to death! Wait, that doesn't sound good. But hey! It says you can, like, probably fix it by, um, by. . . Hmm. I don't understand most of this stuff. I think you have to go outside to do it. *(to self)* I didn't know you could go out into space.

Astronaut #1

Damn it! I'm in no mood to go out there

Astronaut #2

I refuse to do anything until we've got this whole thing with your wife settled, Fulton.

Astronaut #3

I'll do it I guess
Your bickering is dreadful
Let me end my stress

Astronaut #1

Fantastic!
(Begins pushing #3 towards the back right of the stage)
You go and we'll stay. You do know what you're doing? Of course you do, we all do. Go on now, go. We don't have all day. Have fun.
(#3 exits the stage. A sharp hiss indicates the closing of the air lock)
I don't like him much.

Astronaut #2

Now Fulton, back to your wife. Are you ready to hammer this all out?

Astronaut #1

Absolutely. You can have her.

Astronaut #2
May I? Truly?

Astronaut #1
Certainly. I was only keeping her around out of convenience anyway.
Although I must admit I suspect I will miss having a wife.

Astronaut #2
Well if all goes as planned and your brother doesn't pose any
significant threat. . .

Astronaut #1
Oh he won't. He's quite the pushover. Very unlike me if not for the
looks.

Astronaut #2
In that case, my wife may be single quite soon.

Astronaut #1
Your wife *is* attractive. Do you think I might have a shot with her?

Astronaut #2
She has always been fond of you.

Astronaut #1
How excellent! Everything is solved. Now let's go check on our
young Ash and see how he's doing.
(They walk to the right of the stage and mimic peering out a window)
There he is.

Astronaut #2
Yes, and he's waving *(starts waving back)*. Hello Ash!

Astronaut #3
(over the intercom)
Hello my false friends
These lives are but hollow shells
Now witness our ends

Astronaut #2
Always a pleasure speaking with you Ash, *(turning to #1 and #1 turn to
look at #2)* what do you suppose he means?

Astronaut #1
How should I know, I never listen to a word he says. *(turning back to look outside)* Hmm. He appears to be shoving those tools off into space.

Astronaut #2
Doesn't he need those to fix what he's fixing?

Astronaut #1
That was my understanding.

Astronaut #2
Perhaps he is finished then?

Astronaut #1
Now he appears to be detaching himself from the shuttle.

Astronaut #2
Ah, so he is coming back in. Well done Ash! Wait, what's that he's doing now?

Astronaut #1
I believe he is taking off his helmet.

Astronaut #2
Am I mistaken or doesn't he need that to live.

Astronaut #1
That's what I've been told, although I've never been out there without one so it may just be a viscous rumor.

Astronaut #2
I think he must have forgotten. We should remind him. *(starts over towards one of the control panels)*

Astronaut #1
No need for that, his helmets is off.

Astronaut #2
Well is he. . .

Astronaut #1
Dead? Oh yes, very dead.

(#2 returns to his seat and presses a button or flicks a switch)

Astronaut #2
Mission Control?

Mission Control
This is Mission Control and, like, who's this?

Astronaut #2
It's Booker.

Mission Control
And you would be?

(#1 returns to his seat)

Astronaut #2
One of the astronauts.

Mission Control
The space guys! Yeah so, like, how're things? Did you get that temperature thingy fixed?

Astronaut #1
Not exactly. The one we sent out there is currently dead and he threw all the tools into space.

Mission Control
Wow, that's, like, a total bummer.

Astronaut #2
So what should we do?

Mission Control
You could try to come back down here, you know, to earth. But, um, without working temperature stuff you'll burn up.

Astronaut #1
There's nothing else?

Mission Control
Nope. Looks like you guys are, like, totally boned.

Astronaut #1
(With great frustration and contempt and more to himself than anything)
How in Christ's name did you get your job?

Mission Control
Omigod! That is, like the greatest story ever. See I was all –

Astronaut #1
Oh, you think I'm actually interested in anything you have to say.
Sorry, but no. Now if you would kindly shut up so Booker and I could
get back to dying, that would be just great.

Mission Control
That's okay; I've got to go anyway. Hot date, you know. Have fun up
there and I'll see you guys around!

(#1 and #2 stand up and meet halfway between seats)

Astronaut #1
So here we are at the end. Fire or ice, which do you fancy?

Astronaut #2
I've never much liked the heat.

Astronaut #1
Nor I. *(they stand silently for a moment)* Booker, may I hold you?

Astronaut #2
Only if I may hold you.
(They embrace one another)
I believe I would like to kiss you.

Astronaut #1
And I believe I would be insulted if you didn't

*(At this point the flickering lights should begin flickering between several
different colors and the pulses should increase in speed as the scene continues.
Re-enter #3 from the right of the stage, arms outstretched and palms turned
upward. #1 and #2 let go of each other and look towards #3)*

166

Astronaut #2
Why Ash! How lovely to see you no longer dead.

Astronaut #3
I, like the Jesus,
Have resurrected myself
To help, and save us

Astronaut #1
How splendidly convenient and also I think I'm a bit gay *(hugs #2 again)*.

(The fairies re-enter from the left of the stage)

Fairy Girl the first
Would you look at the lot! Two perfectly beautiful fairies standing right here and they choose each other.

Fairy Girl the second
I'd be reasonably insulted if we weren't so perfectly beautiful.

Fairy Girl the first
And just look at this place up here

Fairy Girl the second
Everything up here is so very empty

Fairy Girl the first
You can't very well be full of beauty and empty at the same time

Fairy Girl the second
But we're still beautiful

Fairy Girl the first
Perfectly beautiful. And we have wings.

Fairy Girl the second
I love our wings. Why humans haven't learned to grow wings is something I'll never understand

Fairy Girl the first
Space shuttles, honestly.
(Fairies exit the left of the stage)

Astronaut #2
It seems likes it's time to get on with things.

Astronaut #3
Yes! Come men of space
Let us finish our mission
With speed and with grace

(The three head back towards their seats and as they do the lights stop flickering and dim except for the soft blue spotlight on #3. As he sits, his is the only light. He resumes a blank stare out into nothing and the lights come back on revealing #1 and #2 again. The color lights that had been illuminating the astronauts since the beginning are now completely gone. Everyone is silent for a moment. #3 is the one to break the silence)

Astronaut #3
Isn't there ever anything to do up here?

Astronaut #1
What? Up here?

Astronaut #2
Not really. You can sit a lot.

Astronaut #3
Oh, well that's quite a drain.

Astronaut #1
You get used to it.

Astronaut #2
For the most part.

(Lights fade on all but #3 then that light too soon fades to black)

For Getting Things of Love, I Can't Remember

His name is Johnny. It's not a very unique name, which reflects him well enough. There were times in his life when he thought that had he been given a more interesting name that perhaps he could have grown into a more interesting person. Mostly though he dismissed those thoughts knowing that there's more to a person than their name.

Johnny lives a bland life to be sure. He has a routine. Every morning he wakes up to his alarm clock at 6:51 a.m. He eats the same bowl of cereal and then brushes his teeth. He gets dressed and goes to work. It's a job he is moderately indifferent towards. He shows up on time, works until it's time to leave and gets paid for it, thus allowing his routine to continue for yet another week.

With work done Johnny comes home to his apartment, a small studio number. There's a bed that is also a couch, a television, a bookshelf that is mostly bare, a refrigerator, a toaster, and a microwave. It's all he needs. The only decorations are a single framed painting (or a print of one at least) that he doesn't know the name of and, sitting in his almost empty book case, a slinky. The slinky is hardly a decoration; however it is so glaringly out of place that Johnny doesn't know what else to think of it. He doesn't even know why he has it other than it found its way into the box that held his half dozen books when he moved in. He rarely touches it. What's the point? Johnny can only remember one time he ever felt compelled to play with a slinky, and it wasn't even his.

He had been at a party. Just over a year ago. It was a phase he was going through, attempting to force change upon himself. To be a different person. The party was at a coworker's place. Johnny didn't know him very well but had been nice enough to invite Johnny along. There were a couple dozen people there, although it felt like more in the small apartment. It was nothing extravagant; nothing special. A little bit of music mixed with a lot of talking and drinking.

Johnny watched a small group of people as they exchanged names. Ryan and Danielle and Katie and Ben and Logan. He listened to their conversation that went from movies to politics to books and so on. It flowed seamlessly. Johnny wished to be a part of that. He especially liked Katie. Danielle was voluptuous but Katie was pretty. Her voice was soft. He wanted to go over there, but felt like he'd be intruding. Instead he noticed a little trinket on the coffee table he was standing near. It was a slinky and it reminded him of his home. Without realizing it, Johnny picked up the slinky and began to slink it back and forth between his hands. The rhythmic *slink-slank* of the slinky made him feel at home. A thing that was odd considering Johnny couldn't remember a single time he'd ever taken his own slinky off his bookshelf.

Beneath the sound between his hands Johnny heard the conversation drift to its next topic and suddenly he had something he desperately wanted to say. Something that he needed to say. But he had been standing in his corner for so long that he wasn't quite sure how to interject. He wondered how he should word it. He wondered if anyone would be as amused as he was by it. He wondered if they would even care. He figured they wouldn't. His time had passed, he thought and went back to the slinky.

He stood there for a while yet. He even thought he saw Katie smile at him. It was the best smile he had ever seen. It had to be meant for someone else. Watching as the slinky flowed from one hand to the other, much like he had watched the conversation of those strangers flow from one topic to the next, he stood his ground. Eventually his nose itched and when he scratched the itch away he realized that his hands smelled like slinky. Dirty and metallic. So he went to wash it away.

In the bathroom he decided it was time to leave the party, and the entire party scene, behind. He was no good at this.

Johnny jumped back into his tedious routine without hesitation. Change is too hard in Johnny's estimation. He thinks his life isn't so bad. But while he may not be miserable Johnny doesn't have his happiness. He chose the slinky instead.

Johnny's happiness is called Cady. Or rather that's her name. It is, coincidentally, a name that also means happiness. To call it anything other than a coincidence would be to detract from everything else Cady is. Which is to say, while she may be Johnny's happiness, she is a person as well. Cady is the unremarkably pretty young woman that people pass by everyday and rarely take much notice to. Unless they see her smile. When she smiles she shines.

Cady is the girl who, in high school, decided to be a street magician just because she knew how and who stopped because she forgot how much fun she had. Cady wants to be a scientist and Cady wants to paint. Cady isn't looking to change the world, but she wouldn't mind it if she did.

By the time she's thirty she'll have created a painting that will revolutionize the way art is perceived. By the time she's thirty she'll have helped make a major break though in fighting cancer. By the time she's thirty she could have done anything. Cady just wants to enjoy her life.

She has always been popular; has had her share of boyfriends. She found them all too predictable. She wants someone who she doesn't understand; who can surprise her. Someone who when she told him about her street magic wouldn't ask to see a trick. He would just make a flower appear and put in her hair. Except not that because she's already thought of it. Something completely different and unexpected.

She realizes she could wait her whole life and never have it happen, so she still dates and is still unimpressed. She still goes to parties just to see what there is to see. At a party just about a year before is the only time Cady recalls being taken off guard. What she remembers most is how simple it was.

It had been a Friday night and she found herself in an apartment with plenty of other people. She didn't know who lived there, some friend of a friend of a friend. It didn't much matter; there were drinks and music and people, after all.

She eventually found herself mixed in with a smaller group of people discussing god knows what. Occasionally she would look up and away from her little group and notice the guy standing all alone in a corner near a table. He was just standing at first until the time that he wasn't. Then he was standing there playing with a slinky.

It thrilled her probably more than it should have, even more than she'd ever admit to herself. There he was surrounded by a dozen people and somehow completely alone. Just him and his slinky. It occurred to her that maybe she should find it sad, but she refused to believe it anything less than adorable.

She watched him out of the corner of her eye, glancing towards him from time to time. There was a moment when she was sure that he was about to abandon his slinky and come talk to her and she was almost giddy. What would he say? But she never found out. He didn't speak. He didn't even move.. And then a little later someone yelled her name. Even as she turned to address the voice, she had made up her mind to go and talk to Mr. Slinky (for that's what she had dubbed him in her mind), but as she turned and began her approach she saw that he had done something completely unexpected. He had vanished. And no one knew where he went. As far as most were concerned he hadn't even been there. It was the kind of moment she had been waiting for. Except that in her mind she always assumed he'd come back.

This is how it was meant to happen:

Johnny hears the conversation take its turn and he quietly approaches the group and tells them what had come to his mind. Cady laughs. In part because what was said was funny and in part because she had already developed something of a crush on the shy man with the slinky.

Cady and Johnny talk the rest of the night. Continue to talk long after that night has passed. Cady does most of the talking and Johnny the listening. Occasionally she is surprised when he gets so impassioned by a subject that he goes on for hours. She surprises him every time she calls.

And then they are in love.

And Cady doesn't understand.

And Johnny has his happiness.

This is how it was meant to happen.

But that's not the way it is. Johnny and Cady are in their routines. One is more enjoyable than the other. They live their lives.

Both might be surprised at the number of near misses they've had since that party. Walking down opposite sides of the same street at the same time. Buying groceries at the same store, only separated by an aisle or two. A trip to the bank only 10 minutes apart.

Still, there is one place where they connect.

They dream.

They dream of how it could have been. How it should have been.

Hushed days spent in bed because it's raining outside.

Because Cady (Johnny) is sick

Because it's warm

Because it's where they want to be

Picnics on the floor of Johnny's (their) apartment. She didn't know he could cook. Neither did he.

She loves it when he cooks. He knows she does.

He lets her cut his hair. They are both surprised by how good it turns out. She offers to let him cut hers. He gets nervous and says no.

She knew he would.

He's so predictable.

She doesn't mind.

She loves the theatre.

He loves her.

He loves quiet nights at home.

She loves him.

This is how it could have been. How it should have been.

They wake up never remembering anything. At best they have a soft sense of longing. Of loss. Mostly though, they feel nothing. And they live their lives.

It's a Saturday. Late morning. Johnny is going to the bank.

It's a Saturday. Almost noon. Cady is going to the bank.

Johnny enters the bank. He sneezes. He's still getting over his cold from last week. The bank door closes behind him and he pauses, feeling like he shouldn't be here. Knowing that he shouldn't. Then he sneezes again and it's gone. Whatever it was. The bank door opens and . . .

Cady enters the bank. And suddenly she feels sick. Or she

174

feels like she should feel sick. She shouldn't be here.

She's in bed and she's coughing. Johnny had a cold and he gave it to her. He always does this. Such a bastard. Then there he is with her soup. She didn't ask for soup but of course it's for her. She loves his soup. She smiles. She smiles because he loves it. And she coughs again. And it's wet and she's too warm and it hurts. But she's sick and it passes. She eats her soup and Johnny says he should go to the bank but she says that he can't because she's sick and it's his entire fault. He has to stay because she's sick because

She's not sick. Not now. She just got a little lightheaded for a second. It happens. Then Cady sees a man in front of her who looks familiar. And she's pretty sure it's Mr. Slinky from that party way back when. How exciting!

She's going to talk to him when the screaming starts. Then she sees the gun. Then she sees the other gun. The bank is being robbed and people are screaming and Cady is trying not to laugh because

Johnny thought this kind of thing only happened in the movies. He wonders if maybe these bank robbers had seen all the movies he had. And he's laughing in spite of the screams. He's laughing but no one notices.

The men with the guns tell everyone to sit down and not to move. They tell everyone to keep their mouths shut or they'll be shot. This will all be over soon.

And Johnny thinks that they look strung out.

And Cady wonders who would get high before robbing a bank.

And they both sit down right next to each other. Cady on Johnny's right and Johnny on Cady's left. Johnny glances over. He recognizes her. She had been at that party where all he did was play with a slinky. She had been part of that group he was listening to and wanted to talk to. He wanted to talk to her most of all. He thinks her

175

name might be Katie. He says nothing. First out of the fear of being shot, second because he's sure she wouldn't recognize him. Or maybe it's the other way.

Things get quiet and Cady sits thinking about how she's going to talk to the guy sitting next to her as soon as this is over. She thinks that a bank robbery has to be a good ice breaker.

Johnny just can't wait to get home. This is why he doesn't like going out. If it's not a bank robbery it's something else. He keeps his eyes to the ground and notices Katie's shadow as she picks up her purse and starts to twirl it. It's slow and it's graceful and

Cady doesn't even realize that she's doing it. Some sort of nervous habit she never knew she had. Until she drops it.

It's louder than it should be. That's what they both think. A lot of people get scared. One of them has a gun. Everything is slower now. Cady and Johnny both close their eyes at the same time. Neither is sure why they are doing it, except that they are expecting something that they'd rather not see. Then the tiny explosion sounds off. A gun is fired. Johnny feels his heart jump and his breath catch in his throat, but nothing else.

Cady feels her chest collapse.

And it's wet.

And it's warm.

And then it starts to hurt.

And her face is wet, but as she opens her eyes she realizes those are just tears. When did she start crying? She can't remember. She hears screaming from all around her. She thinks she must be doing it, but she's not. She's trying. She can't. But everyone else can. And everyone else is, she notices as she looks around. Everyone else, except for the man right next to her on her left. The guy from that party so long ago. Her Mr. Slinky. And for the first time today he is looking directly at her.

And for the first time today she is looking directly at him. Johnny sees the tears on her face. He sees her life running red from beneath her. Running towards him. Soaking through his jeans to get to his skin. And her life touches him.

And it's wet.

And it's warm.

And then it starts to hurt.

He doesn't have time to wonder why because this girl who is dying next to him, whose name might have been Katie, whose life had just touched him in a way that no one's had nor ever would again, this girl is trying

To think of something to say. Cady wants to know whatever she can about this boy, this young man sitting next to her. What is his name? What does he do? Where is he from? Anything. Because in a very real way he is the closest person to her heart at this moment, and she just knows she has to say something. So she finds herself saying the natural thing. Cady says hi to Johnny.

She says it more sweetly than she has a right to. Because her lungs are filling with blood. Because she is drowning. Yet she sounds as she would in most any other situation. Just like Cady. Then she smiles. Not a big smile, although she tries. Her teeth remain hidden behind her lips, which is for the best since they are now stained by blood not content with being confined to her lungs. But despite the blood pouring from her nose now and the tiny trickles of blood that escape from each corner of her mouth it's a pretty smile.

And so Johnny says the only thing that he can think to say. He says hi back.

Then Cady is dead. Or perhaps she already was. And Johnny just sits there feeling her life soak into him even after she is gone.

And it's still wet.

And it's still warm.

And it's sticky and it's gross, but he sits there still. He sits there through the screaming. He sits there through more gunshots. He keeps sitting there until someone comes and tells him it's okay to leave. He sits there because she should never have to know.

The rest of the day goes by in a blur. The police are there and they escort everyone out. Johnny sees all the crying faces and notices he isn't one of them. He doesn't know why. He's at the police station answering questions for paperwork that's to be filled out by someone else. There's not going to be a trial because the police had no choice but to kill the robbers. Johnny is okay with this.

Then somehow he is home.

He doesn't remember how he got there, but it's dark now and he's tired and he doesn't care. The first thing he notices upon entering is the slinky resting in his bookcase. And suddenly he no longer wants it there. He picks it up telling himself he's getting rid of it. What good is it anyway? But all he does is let it teeter from one hand to the other. He sits on his bed and watches it and listens to the rhythmic *slink-slank*. Aware of how much he hates the sound. Hating it because of the comfort he finds in it, but not stopping just the same.

He continues for a long time until it makes one final slink out of his hand and collects itself in perfect slinky fashion on the floor.

Motionless, Johnny sleeps.

There are no dreams.

Cancer

The bar is empty save for a group of two men and a woman sitting at a table near the very back; another older man at the end of the bar, nearest the friendly group; the bartender and me, of course. Outside was cold, every breath a plume of smoke. I just don't want to be cold anymore.

I'm too young to have any olfactory memories of bars laced with cigarette smoke encircling the scent of liquor and sweat. Yet I still expect it as I sit down and am disappointed by its absence. I couldn't say why. I've never smoked in my life.

I choose the stool closest to the entrance and eventual exit; furthest away from all the others. My notes are still with me from earlier in the day so I set them on the bar next to me. I'm halfway through scanning my surroundings before I realize I'm looking for a clock. Not finding one I look at my watch, wondering why I didn't just do that in the first place. The time is 11:47 pm.

I need a beer.

The bartender obliges in short order and then leaves me to sit and drink and poke around my notes. Even though I record my interviews, by video or cassette depending on what I'm allowed, I make sure everything is handwritten. When I write things out it feels more certain.

I guess machines just make me uncomfortable.

The purpose of these interviews I'm not exactly sure. I'm not much of a writer and don't know a thing about filmmaking. If I had to put forth a reason I'd say for peace of mind.

It was a few years ago that I went and got tested. Or maybe analyzed is a better term. A short time later I was given a piece of paper that read only, "**CANCER**". The Death Machine had told me I would die of cancer.

There's terror in that word, but dread wasn't my initial reaction. It was disappointment. Of all the ways to die, I get cancer. It was obvious. It was ordinary. It was boring. The implications of that tiny piece of paper, that single word, didn't sink in until I tried to sleep. I couldn't.

Things started to change. It was a bunch of small stuff. I started spending less time with my friends who smoked, telling myself it was just because I was busy. Eventually I just didn't see them anymore. I spent more time on the Internet, always researching the latest in cancer news. What might cause what and how best not to get it. And I started visiting my doctor with greater frequency.

It was awhile before I let myself notice what I was doing to my life. The effect my diagnosis had on me was undeniable, but I didn't want to think about me so I turned my thoughts to everyone else. Anyone else. Why? Well I think I just didn't want to be alone. That's how the interviews started.

Most of them are just of local people giving their two cents; nothing special. I have a dozen interviews with doctors explaining how the money has never been better. There's another five with local religious leaders. Faith is huge these days with most people seeing the machine as clear proof of God's existence. Something about how he's written our stories in our blood. Church leaders are happy about the record attendance they are seeing. Although a few worry that people are attending for the wrong reasons they, for the most part, don't let it get the best of them. My favorite quote was from the pastor of the Presbyterian Church two blocks from my apartment. He said, "I cannot concern myself with why everyone first walks through our doors, I can only concern myself with why they continue to come back." Still I've only ever had one noteworthy interview, and that was today.

I met Gareth Ryder early this afternoon. It was a last minute thing that was completely unexpected. I never thought I'd get to interview him. Especially not today. So it's not a surprise that I dropped everything. Only a few miles separated us, so I walked. I passed a small group of protestors in order to enter the building. There signs read "**Freedom, not Fate**" and "**God's Will is our Free Will**". Even though I wore a heavy coat it was still too cold inside.

Gareth was a good looking kid and really that's all he was, a kid. Light brown hair, faded blue eyes, soft features; it's not how I imagined him. He offered a polite smile and although we don't shake hands I can't help but observe he kept his immaculately. I asked if we could jump right into it and he nodded slightly. My first question was, "when did you get tested?"

"Tested?" he asked back, a bit confused. "Test - I don't . . . I mean, are you talking about the death machine?" I nod and wait for him to continue. "Right, sorry of course you are. I just—I have a lot on my mind and I talk to too many people. I guess – I guess I was 16? Yeah, yeah I was 16. I went with a group of friends. We all decided to go because I had my license and we, well I guess we thought it would be fun."

"Fun?" I interjected, trying to sound like a real journalist, a façade that didn't last long.

"Well, sure it was . . . this was almost immediately after the machine was first released, you know, to the public. We'd heard all about it. How it was supposedly real. I mean that what it said or told you was real. Like it really happened, but to us it was like this big myth. An urban legend or something. So we just figured we'd get a big kick out of it. And we did too, at first. The trip there was short, but we were excited. There was me and my friends, Aimee, Evan, and Jason.

"We went to one of those, I don't know what you call them, street vendors, I guess. Do you know what I'm talking about? Those people who somehow got a hold of a machine and offer to give you your analysis for cheap, sometimes even free? I don't think many are left since the machines are everywhere now, but this was near the beginning. Either way it was better than going to a doctor's office where we might need parental consent. Anyway, that's where we went.

"It was pretty quick, but I'm sure you know all about the process. Jason went first. His said, "**DRUNK DRIVING**". We all joked about how we'd never drive with him again while I got mine done." He paused there and I wasn't sure he would continue, but neither did I want to push him into it. I was about to prompt him when he started up again.

"I don't know what I was expecting when I got that paper. I actually had to read it two or three times before it made any sense to me, but when I finally did I got this . . . this sort of jolt. You know how it is when it feels like something's caught in your chest and it kind of hurts? But I had to say something because I knew everyone was watching me and waiting. I told them it said heart failure. It really wasn't that big of a lie. It was too boring for anyone to want to see it right away which is what I was banking on. I was able to slip it into my wallet and that's where it stayed until my wallet was taken from me.

Aimee was next and she had a very visible frown when she read her paper. She showed it to us. It read "**BEST FRIEND**". That thing in my chest took hold again, but only briefly because Evan returned with a diagnosis of "**ANGRY CIRCUS CLOWN**".

"We laughed about it the entire way home."

"And then what happened?" I asked and he surprised me by laughing. It was warmer than I would have guessed.

"That's a pretty vague question," is what he came back with.

I could only say, "Sorry."

"No, no it's fine. Most people are so specific with what they want to hear about that I end up telling the same thing over and over. What happened after the Death Machine? I went home and put it out of my mind. And I kept it out, for the most part, until my second year in college. That's when Aimee was in her accident.

"Maybe I should explain first that Aimee's parents died when we were both ten. Severe food poisoning if you can believe that. Our families were friends and my parents ended up taking her in after that. We were always close, Aimee and I. Still, I was surprised to find out she had a will made up and even more surprised that I was named executor. It was touching really. And that's how I came to kill my best friend.

"The doctor's said she would never wake up. Nevertheless I waited as long as I could stand. And then I waited another week. But eventually I let her let go. Listening to the rhythm of her life go flat, surrounded by machines, I could see in my mind a slip of paper singing **BEST FRIEND** monotonously. **BEST FRIEND** became another two words, my words. I was relieved until I was terrified."

He stopped like he was waiting for me to interject, to say anything, but I was never much of an interviewer. I was only good at listening. When it became apparent that I had no intention of speaking he continued.

"This is where I turn to drugs, heroin to be specific. I wish it didn't sound so cliché, but I tend to be more bothered by how worried I can be about sounding cliché. Something like that really shouldn't matter, but I can't help it.

"The heroin wasn't about a depression over Aimee's death," he paused putting his left hand to his mouth and vise versa. Trying to

183

collect his thoughts into words he bit down on his middle knuckle. Part of me worried for that immaculate hand. "What it was, what I think it was about, was that Aimee's death had come from her best friend so I had to kill myself to satiate the Death Machine. That's why I chose heroin. It had to be that way. Aimee's death made that clear enough.

"Only it didn't work, obviously. Not that I didn't do my best, but after my fourth overdose with no noticeable damage of any kind I consented that heroin wasn't a way out. I cleaned up with the delirious hope that withdrawal might end me, knowing full well that it couldn't.

"The drugs behind me, I went back out into the world. I got back into my life. Nothing much to speak of, one day I went to a bar and now I'm here. That's that."

"I-I, um, well," my words stumble over my tongue, fearful the interview has ended, but he saves me just a quickly as I faltered.

"Don't worry I'm not done," he reassured. "I was just screwing around. It wasn't all that satisfying.

"So there was this bar and there was this girl. That's where I was, right?" He didn't wait for a response, just kept on, "The only reason I approached her was that she looked how I felt, a little bit sad and alone.

"She was 23, only a couple of years older than me. Lenore, that's what she said her name was. Mine's Gareth, that's what I told her. This, I don't know, funny sort of look seeped into her face when I said that. And her voice shook when she asked for my last name. Before I even finished saying Ryder I saw her change. She went silent. She had already stopped talking, but her body went still. There were tears at the beds of her eyes. I expected them to burst through, but they only rested there. She never cried. Not then, not later.

"Maybe I knew at that moment, with hindsight it's hard to say. But when she asked to see my driver's license I didn't question it. She looked it over for a long time. When she finally did hand me something back, it wasn't my license. Instead it was a very familiar sliver of paper. And like all those important to me it had two words printed on it. **GARETH RYDER** is what it read."

"And then . . ." I started.

"And then I showed her my paper. She read it. We both understood enough. Then I killed her." He said flatly.

"It-it was that simple?"

"Yes," he said it with no hesitation, "but maybe no also. We talked for awhile. She told me all about the fear she held ever since first reading my name on that paper. We shared our failed suicide attempts. She told me she was glad that I was so nice. And then we resolved to kill each other. So, in the end, it was that simple.

"I know how unbelievable it sounds, two people just acquiescing to their respective deaths so easily, but that's how it happened. I'm not sure I can explain the comfort that we found in finally being able to take control of this thing that had controlled our lives for so long. It was a relief. That's the best I can do.

"We went out to an empty parking lot and sat around discussing how best to go about the whole thing. I told her it had to look violent; I said to her, 'you have to understand it needs to look violent, it needs to look real,' that's what I said. And she just nodded. She was dreadfully accommodating and made it very easy on me. I tried my best to make it easy on her too. I tried.

I didn't know how to start so she took my hands in hers. She held them for too long before saying 'You have beautiful hands'. Those were her last words, you have beautiful hands. Then she put them around her throat. It's a lot harder to strangle someone than you might think. It took longer than I wanted. I know when her last breath escaped her because it was cold that night.

"Afterwards I, uh, there was a loose piece of pavement so I . . . I thought it needed to look violent and . . . well anyway it didn't take too long for them to find me. She had my name with her after all. The trial was quick. I never said a word. As it turns out the most damning bit of evidence was this," he managed to push a tiny piece of paper my way. I took it in my hands but never really looked at it. "You can keep that," he continued. "I don't need it anymore. Anyway the judge, and jury I guess, basically said that if I could still commit such a crime then I only deserved the harshest of punishments. So it all worked out, you know.

"You're wondering why, right? That's the question you want to ask, just like those people outside. It's simple, actually. The reason I didn't defend myself, that I rejected all appeals, is because it has to be this way. Otherwise my dying thought would only be that she didn't have to die, not then. Not because of me. Waking every day to that possibility is hard enough. I can't die with it.

"Besides, the machine is never wrong so why struggle. All it does is make you tired in the end. And I'm already exhausted."

We sat in silence after that. Not for too long, a minute at most. Finally he said, "Look, I've got to go. Busy day today and I still have my big dinner to get ready for." He laughed and it was still friendly and warm. He was escorted out, and so I left and walked. I walked for a long time.

Eventually I found myself here, slowly spinning an almost empty glass. I consider finishing it, but it wasn't very fulfilling. Besides, I need air. So I pay for my drink and gather up my notes. Outside it's still cold. I'm breathing smoke again, much like a woman settled a few buildings down. Only hers is real. She looks calm. She looks warm. I just don't want to be cold anymore.

I have to walk her way to get home, that's my excuse. My

approach is anxious and would be worse if she were watching. I ask if I can bum a smoke. Afraid I'll be too timid; I overcompensate by being too loud. There's a pause where she gives me a looking over. I have time enough to wonder if I should be embarrassed about saying "bum a smoke", but not time enough to actually settle into that discomfiture as she almost immediately hands me a cigarette. Rolling it between my fingers she asks if I need a light. I nod and say thank you. The tiniest warmth emanates from her finger tips and I inhale deeply.

I exhale in a fit of violent coughs. My benefactor smirks, almost laughing at my inexperience. Trying not to appear a novice I assure her that I'm getting over a serious cold. She doesn't seem interested in my lies. I feel foolish and take another deep breath.

The results are much the same and my mouth tastes like cinder, but still I swear to her that it's just my cold. I continue to press this point even as she extinguishes her cigarette and saunters off into the night. Her smoky breaths the last bit taken by the dark.

I don't give up with her gone. The third drag is better than the previous two. I still cough, but less. And this time there's warmth permeating throughout my chest. I practice breathing smoke and I get better. Just before it's finished it feels comfortable.

I watch as a tiny paper flutters from my notes. It's Gareth's death slip. Kneeling down, I read it for the first time. I already know what it'll say. I take one last breath. And then drop the cigarette on Gareth's fate.

I start to walk again. Noting my surroundings unenthusiastically. The streets are all but empty, save for me of course. I check my watch. The time is 12:19 am. At 12:01 am Gareth Ryder was executed by means of **LETHAL INJECTION**.

I'm cold again.

I need another cigarette.

PREVIEWS

IT BEGAN 70 MILES SOUTHWEST OF ATHENS . . . GEORGIA.

HIGH ATOP THE OLYMPIC STADIUM IN ATLANTA.

FORGED FROM A METAL MOST MALLEABLE. PLASTIC.

THE ROBORACLE COMETH.

FROM HIS MIGHTY BEGINNINGS TO A STARTLING FUTURE.

ALL SECRETS SHALL BE REVEALED.

ALL BUT ONE.

AND THEN THAT ONE TOO.

LIFE. DEATH. THESE ARE JUST WORDS.

WORDS KNOWN BY **THE ROBORACLE**.

ASK THE FATES IN 2008!

-PREVIEW-

STEEL CANYON

It was a Tuesday. That I remember. My sleep was delicate as dawn neared. Nightmares of work loomed on the periphery of my dreams, forcing me awake earlier than I preferred to face the entirely worse reality of it all. I glanced out the window. The first light of day was a jeweler's exhibition in layers; ruby, amethyst, and sapphire.

I showered reluctantly. Knowing it was only part one in a pedantic routine that would eventually lead me into the city and a job that was leisurely worsening my sanity. Ten minutes before I was scheduled to exit my apartment and take those next necessary steps towards mental breakdown my phone rang. I almost didn't answer it, having become so accustomed to a routine that didn't involve a ringing phone. Against my better judgment, as well as the sadist within me begging for another step towards complete lunacy, I acquiesced to the phones demands.

My friend Lacy barely let me get out a hello before berating me with news of the beautiful day that had offered itself up for praise. As if she didn't trust my mind to process what my eyes were seeing. Several minutes passed and I was getting anxious, but Lacy only reminded me of all my complaints of the last two years. I was trying to grasp her reasoning in starting her day with such negativity, especially directed at me, when she asked me to skip work. Lacy didn't work in the city. Had never even visited. Her point became clear. I had worked in the city for two years yet had never walked the streets. I took the transit straight to my building. Rarely looked up. "The Steel Canyon must be spectacular today," said Lacy, her daydreams palpable even over the phone. There was no saying no without crushing a bit of her. I couldn't allow her to become like me, not in the slightest.

The city is called the Steel Canyon for two reasons. The first is literal and architectural. The financial district is lined for miles with skyscrapers of equal height. From the outside they appear to onlookers as a flat, shining steel wall. This illusion is nothing spectacular when you consider it's produced by the reflective windows mimicking what stands opposite them. A giant, equidistance, shining steel wall. The wall was built to separate the financial district from the slums. The idea being that staring at a wall was better for morale than death and sickness. Unfortunately the wall only reflects what it was built to hide.

If you stand upon one of the building's roofs it's as if you are looking down into a grand steel canyon. It's impossible to escape.

And there's the second meaning.

The only way out is death or madness. An entire populace's despair gets left at the bottom. Still, on the outside, as a tourist, on that Tuesday, it was breathtaking.

Lacy transformed into a child. Dwarfed by the magnitude of the city; awed.

It was shortly before noon when the air ignited. It all happened in seconds. Fractions of seconds. The last thing I remember is her smile, before a river of fire surged through the Canyon. I had time enough for one last breath. A gasp that combusted in my mouth; down my throat, exploding the surviving remnants of oxygen in my lungs. They expanded excruciatingly. To the point of bursting. Yet they held.

I tasted embers. Breathed fire.

Panicking, I turned to Lacy. Although the flash was blinding, in that moment the shadow of her smile, illuminating, scorched its silhouette forever in the dark behind my eyes. And as I felt her hand in mine, changing from flesh to ash, I knew what I was. What I had to become.

The fire burned itself out and I stood alone.

STEEL CANYON

-Preview-

THE CHRONOLOGICAL ADVENTURES OF PANIK THE TIME-HOPPING HUMAN SEX-BOT AND HER SERPENTINE SHARD OF SADISTIC LOVE

Her trips through time were one too many and her robotic heart was failing; she would persist.

Look for more
Chronological Adventures
IN TIME!

-Preview-

CANDY KISSES AND BULLET HOLES
FILL HER UP

My name is Victor, and I'm a slave.

It wasn't always like this. But then along came a girl.

Emma.

I met her when people's nightmares started to come to life. Or at least that's what I thought was happening. But I was wrong. Dead wrong. In reality, the Triple-verse had begun to bleed into one. So I burned it down. Everything seemed perfect for awhile, yet it only solved two things. Jack and shit. And Jack just left town. (very original.) I'm 100% original, baby. (yeah right.) Groovy!

For the last sixteen weeks I've found myself in a dire circumstance. Lost in space and, um, enslaved. But that's neither here nor there. This ship's been searching the galaxy for some sort of space whale (fliperisakiss). I don't know what they call it. I don't pay much attention.

There is talk of slave gladiatorial matches at the next port, and a lot of the slaves are preparing. I'm not. I have a foolproof plan. See I'm going to bide my time, relax, wait until the last minute. And then when it seems like all hope is lost I'll get rescued by Emma.

It's flawless.

I hear the latch slide behind the walls, unlocking the heavy door to the holding cage compartment on the Adventure Galley. The crew has also decided to use the space to store their other space-found catches.

Green blood oozes from one large fliperisakiss they have freshly killed while roaming the space-ways. The stench is unbearable.

"….ℏ⬚ℏ↕ ⬚ℏ⬚⬚ ⬚ℏ ℏ ⬚⬚" an alien pirate states as his hand slips from the slimy fliperisakiss' ear lobe. "↕↕⬚⬚ℓ⬚!"

I turn to my neighboring cage, "Well, looks like old Grease Mitts is having his usual meat-handling problems!"

Grease Mitts knocks my cage bars with a stun baton and jars

my self-congratulating inflections of yet again coming up with an innuendo for the circumstance. He speaks galactic basic in a broken tongue, "Air lock out with you! I have no worry!" (galactic basic? It's just English.) But galactic basic sounds more sci-fi. (you mean it sounds more Star Wars.)

"⇕⇕□□_⫏□ !" I yell back at him in his language. I have no idea what I just said but it pisses him off and he lunges the baton through the bars trying to jab me. I deftly shift my mass away and knock the stick out of his hand. He moves away from the cage too fast for me to hit him with the charged baton, but that was never my target to begin with. I drive the baton into the locking mechanism of the cage and the heavy door springs open. Without a full charge on the baton, it's basically worthless, but I take this into account. I throw the recharging baton into the cell of the undefeated gladiatorial slave and direct my attention back to the two alien pirates charging me. I scream my war cry and charge.

They have me pinned to the floor but, as anticipated, have not called for back-up. Out of the corner of my eye I see a swift moving appendage crush down on the back of Grease Mitts' head. He is definitely out for the count. The other alien pirate releases his grip on me and begins backing away from the newly freed gladiatorial slave champion. I slowly get to my feet and wait for the gladiator to turn on me, but as I had predicted, he is focused on the alien pirate who has reached behind his back to pull out a wicked looking blade.

The slaver swiftly severs both the slave arms. Proud of himself he begins to laugh, joyful at the sight. Of course there's a reason why this particular slave is gladiatorial champion. He can regenerate his limbs quite rapidly. The slaver really should know this. I mean I know all about it and I've never even seen it, but these slaver aren't too bright. His stupidity makes his reaction all the more laughable as the slaves arms surge out of his elbows and crush the slaver's face.

I give some congratulations and offer up a high five, but my former neighbor just looks at me silently. So rude. (most of the other slave don't speak English, you know.) None the less, some acknowledgement would be polite. It's just simple courtesy.

We stare at each other awkwardly for awhile before I finally say, "mutiny?" which I take he understands because he's smiling now. Or at least I think it's a smile. His face is very disgusting.

It takes a few minutes, but we free the rest of the slaves and burst out of the slave quarters screaming war cries. (you're the only one screaming anything.) It's called enthusiasm. The rest of the slaves are busy brutalizing anything that gets in their way. I, however, have no time for that. I'm headed straight for the bridge and Captain Valiant.

I get lost a couple times. (but we're here now so what are we waiting for?) Oh, well I have to think of something brilliant to say as I burst through the door. I'm thinking "Hey Captain Valiant! Meet General Mutiny. He's about to court marshal your ass!" (that's awful.) No I think it'll work. I'm going for it.

As I burst onto the bridge, "Hey Captain Valiant! Meet . . . Emma?"

"Hey Vic," What. The. Fuck?

"Ah, a pleasure to meet you," says an unbelievably handsome man sitting next to Emma. "I'm Captain Valiant. And you, clearly, are Victor." He gets up and shakes my hand with all the suaveness of body soap. (nice.) "Victor, now that . . . that is a *valiant* name." And with a smile that's just dashing I . . . why am I here again? (mutiny.) That's just out of the question. I could never stay mad at this man. "Please, have a seat. Emma and I were just discussing terms of your release."

"So when you say negotiating the terms of my release you mean?"

"Oh please," says Emma, "get your mind out of the gutter. We were just trying to figure out which slave quarters you were in."

"But now you've fortuitously found your way to us," says the captain. "Problem solved. Although I must tell you that you slaves do great work and you will be missed."

"Actually, I didn't work at all."

"Oh. Well then it'll be good to be rid of you," there's that smile again. (phenomenal.) But that's unimportant! Emma's here!

"So," I turn to her, "how exactly did you find me?"

"We pieced together a few clues we got from the Roboracle before he disappeared and Jimmy built a space ship. He's down in the engine room talking to some cute engine girl or something. We really need to get going though."

"Why?" (why? Why are you asking why? I thought we wanted off here) Yeah, but Captain Valiant is so cool!

"Candy Island," she says, "we have to get to Candy Island."

"Candy Island," asks Valiant. "That sounds exciting and dangerous. And here on The Adventure Galley we're always looking for *adventure*."

"Yes! Captain Valiant comes with us!" I'm so excited. (too excited really.)

"That's fine," starts Emma. She's so pretty when she's determined," I don't care who comes, but let's go. The fate of the universe rests on Candy Island!"

(maybe we should tell them about the mutiny outside?) Nah, I'm sure it'll work itself out.

To Be Continued!

Autobiography

I was born in the mountains of Kansas in 1977. It was sometime before Friday and Thursday had long since passed away. It was a short yet excruciating process which haunts me to this day. My mother was in Washington and therefore missed the entire thing. This is wholly typical of her. My father, being an automaton, was built several years later out of used vodka bottles and soda cans. To this day he refuses to acknowledge me as his own.

On my fifth birthday, at the lonely age of 12 and 5/9ths, I discovered that I had the ability to see through walls and other wall like structures. This explained all those years of running into things that weren't there. It was also the cause of sights that led to days of unwanted therapy at the hands of my uncle, with special emphasis on the hands. My parents had no siblings which made me suspicious of his claims, but not so much as to end my idle behavior.

Years later I lost my virginity at the prime age of 7. It was unexceptional and the girl spent the total time in another room. It is easily one of the top three moments of my life.

My death came at the hands of my arch-nemesis whom happened to be composed of little more than soot, flour, and carnations. We decided to be arch-nemeses when it was discovered one of us believed Journey to be musical pioneers while the other considered them to be nothing more than a word meaning the act of traveling from one place to another; a trip. We both considered this an unacceptable difference of opinion and decided to devote our respective lives to the destruction of the other. I was successful with little resistance, but I made the mistake of eating my foe. I happened to have a surgical procedure only an hour later. My less than empty stomach was my downfall. Tomorrow I plan on meeting my soul mate.